WHISPERING GEORGE

E.R. BAILLIE

WHISPERING GEORGE

iUniverse books may be ordered through booksellers or by contacting:

iUniverse
1663 Liberty Drive
Bloomington, IN 47403
www.iuniverse.com
844-349-9409

ISBN: 978-1-6632-3567-1 (sc)
ISBN: 978-1-6632-3568-8 (e)

Library of Congress Control Number: 2022902717

Print information available on the last page.

iUniverse rev. date: 02/11/2022

For my siblings Jim, Rossie, Bill and Donald Baillie

Chapter 1

1949

One more train, one more and he'd be home; but first, Cass. George pulled his rucksack from the rack, and stepped down to the platform. He trudged through the foul smoke of the engine and out the station into the city.

The last taxi screeched to a stop. The driver watched through the rear-view mirror as he threw in his rucksack and climbed in behind it.

"Where to, soldier?"

"136 Randall Hill Rd."

The cabby turned with a lop-sided grin on his face. "No need to whisper, soldier. No one else around to hear!"

George looked out the window without answering.

"Hope you saved your pay!" he laughed. He put the car in gear and peeled up Yonge St. but kept talking, always with a streak of tease in his voice, watching in the rear-view mirror for a reaction.

George, not a bit interested in satisfying the man's curiosity, continued to stare out his window, mesmerized by the rush of cars and people and noise. It was like a kid's kaleidoscope; everything and everybody twisted into a buggered-up pattern, so busy moving, honking and screeching that he wondered if the city ever gave the citizens the freedom of quiet, or if they even wanted it. He had left yes sirs and no sirs and rules and hospitals and arrived to confusion; but not for much longer that was for damn sure. Soon he would exhale, on his land, in his place, on the island where he planned to nest for the rest of his life.

Obviously upset by George's silence the driver slammed on his brakes in front of 136 Randall Hill. and didn't turn. George got out and shook his head at the sight of the place. It's huge stone façade emitted a silent superiority, that disguised the activities within.

The driver opened his window "That'll be two dollars!" His tone was brusque.

George turned to the taxi, and reached into his rear pocket for his wallet: the gesture exposed the bandaging around his neck.

The driver's mouth dropped open, and he pointed to George's neck. "That's why you whisper?"

"Shrapnel," George murmured.

"Damn Me! Sorry soldier!"

George waved off his apology and watched as the car pulled away

The taxi driver leaned his head out the car and waved. "You deserve a good time in there!"

He climbed the stairs knowing full well it was not a good time that awaited him within.

At his ring, Hawker opened the small window on the door and his face cracked into a big-lipped smile of recognition. Before he knew it, George had an enormous arm around his shoulder and was pulled into an ornate hall. "Every day Cass, she been hoping today be the day you arrive. She be tickled pink!" He relieved George of his rucksack. "She upstairs. Come!"

As they passed the gaudy living room, he felt sick to his stomach, and climbing the elegant staircase had the urge to cry.

Cassandra, was sitting at her desk and when she saw him standing there unsmiling, she flung back her chair, ran across the room and enveloped him in a strangling hug. He nuzzled his head into her neck and inhaled the familiar perfume of her skin, then stood back and stared at her in wonder. She had cut her hair short and it was dyed almost white which made her startling blue eyes even more disturbing. He laughed at himself. How could he have believed for even one moment that his absence would have at least lightened the weight? Her beauty had dictated his whole life.

"Plumped up a little have you Cass?" he teased. Without the injury, his reply would still have been a croak.

She stepped back, with hands on hips, "Not one ounce and you know it George Brown!"

He pulled her back into his arms, where she belonged even though she couldn't accept it. "You're perfect," he mumbled.

She gently touched the bandage on his neck. "And your voice?"

"I'm going to squawk for the rest of my, life but at least I'm vertical and can talk some."

"Oh Georgie, it's so good to see you. I've been worrying about you for the last five years." Clasping his hand with both of hers she tugged him into the next room and pulled him down on to a sofa, plunking herself beside him. "We have to talk and talk and talk!"

"Whisper, more like it." George smiled.

"You're alive, and you can communicate, and you're here." She kissed his hand and held it to her cheek before lowering it to her lap, but not letting go for a minute.

He had no idea how long they stayed like that, massaging the memories of their shared lives. Scenes flashed through his mind. Two children crouching over polliwogs impatient for them to become frogs as they watched, slipping on the moss-laden flat rocks as they slid shrieking into the lake, swinging from trees, shooting home-made bows and arrows, peeling off the delicious burn off marshmallows and popping it their mouths, before biting the gummy remains off the stick and laughing at the gooey results that pasted their faces. The freedom of childhood, the innocent glow in their hearts before life interfered.

She broke the silence with a looking-back voice. "Those trips back and forth from the island to school in Cedartown were a big part of our life.

'As I remember, if we weren't laughing we were fighting."

"You were an unruly brat!" She tilted her head and smiled a memory. "And would have been kicked out school if I hadn't straightened you out. Don't forget that!"

Even her tease charmed him, dammit. "I know, I know."

"Just had to make you use your right hand and stop that mirror writing with your left." This time her smile was naughty. "And it didn't hurt that before you got it all together, a little manual dexterity convinced the teacher you were smarter than you appeared."

They laughed together but George felt the same old, deep, down hurt.

"You still write with your right hand I hope?"

"Of course!" And it was still like dragging his hand through water. She didn't need to know that he wrote with his left hand when alone and needed to clear the clouds.

Cass rose and stared down at his upturned face. "You still look like a swarthy island boy but talk like an educated man. She traced her fingers gently along the edges of his eyes. "The smile lines are still there but the new ones aren't so happy. Want to talk about it?"

He wished she'd leave her hand there forever. "Nope. I grabbed each bad memory and shoved it down into my shadow. When I get back to the island I'll drown it all in the lake." If it will drown. He had a dreaded fear that the black shape was pursuing him.

"Don't you have nightmares?"

"They'll go when I get to the island."

She dropped her hand, kissed his cheek and stood up. "Time for a drink to celebrate!"

He smiled and stared, soaking in the pleasure of seeing her again. As she crossed the room, her movements were as smooth as mercury. He felt himself sliding right back to where he had always been: to a place where love and anger were in perpetual battles in all his dealings with this dame.

She handed him his drink. "What are you going to do with yourself back on the island?"

"I'll take the Wawanesa out of dry dock and get her going again transporting people to and from the island."

"I suppose you're going to start up your still again?"

"Probably. If the town's still dry."

"It is." She tilted her head with a question. "Why the hell do you do it?"

"There's a pleasure in teasing the law. Can't help it." He shrugged his shoulders. "How do you know the town's still dry?"

"I still get the Cedartown Express. Keeps me up to date."

"Do they ever write anything about the island?"

"Some snarky reporter, Arthur Rhodes, I think he's called, wrote about John when he got out of jail. Reviewed the whole damned thing."

"Arthur Rhodes? That pipsqueak son-of a- bitch. He was a steeple chase jockey who got caught up in an illegal gambling set-up. Cedartown immediately christened him 'Jumper'"

"Cedartown has always had a need to create nicknames for everyone."

"Seems to me the people who tag others with labels think they're from a rung above. I can imagine what they'll do to me with my croak."

"What about me?"

"You don't go back anymore, but if you did they'd probably call you The Merry Madam!"

She laughed. "And they'd be right."

"I'm sure Jumper's sarcasm didn't get through to John. He never did get it when he was insulted." George let his head fall back as he thought of John, the product of copulation between bored cousins when the ice on the island socked them in for too long. The man was muscular and handsome but lacked certain survivor qualities. It wasn't that he was extraordinarily dumb, a touch perhaps. It was more that his basic moral code was difficult to figure out. He'd been sent to prison for burning down the lumber mill, to collect the insurance for the owner. But since it was the owner who paid him to do it, John saw no problem in it. And he was shafted. "It's sad to say, but it was probably good John was incarcerated while I was gone."

"Not a great way to be kept out of trouble, and he's back now"

"Well, at least I'm back now to control his proclivities—at least the worst of them."

"George, your eyes are drooping. Sleep. I'll cover you."

Cass woke him gently and handed him another tumbler with rye.

"How long have I been asleep?".

"A couple of hours."

He moved the blanket aside. "What time is it? I want to catch The Northland at nine o'clock."

"There's still time, and there are a couple of things I want to tell you before you go."

He wiped the sand from his eyes. "Serious?"

"Not yet, but could be," She walked around as she talked, leaving George staring up at her. "A place like this services some damn important people in this town, and that, My Friend, makes it a dangerous game. A lot of them are crooked as hell and they know I know. There will come a day, Georgie, when someone will want to get rid of me and everything in my head." She smiled down at him. "At best, they'll have the house shut down: at worst, they'll try and get rid of me." She went into the office and returned with a sheaf of papers. "So, in case the day comes, I've bought the White Farm on the south end of the island."

He couldn't believe it. "I'll have you back home?" And away from your goddamned money-making pleasures.

She put her flat hand against his chest. "Not so fast! This is all 'just in case'. I'm not giving up this little gold mine unless forced to. But meanwhile, I need your help."

"Tell me."

"The old house on the farm is falling apart. I'm going to send Hawker out there to oversee workers who I hired from the other side of the lake."

"That's about 13 miles instead of 3 miles from Cedartown. Doesn't seem logical."

"Does to me. It's privacy I'll want, not the gossip of people who've grown up around me."

"What can I do?"

"Be there for Hawker and be my middle man. Hawker can't read or write."

Cassandra held his coat for him. "I'll write. I'm also sending a lot of papers to you. A copy of my power of attorney for you, just in case things get rough."

Five years away and she still could ask anything of him. He shook his head, smiled a wan smile, and said with an affectionate voice, "You worry me Cassandra, but then, when haven't you?"

"I'm just covering my ass and you are my one true friend."

As he grabbed his rucksack she said, "Oh yes, I forgot to mention, you've finally got a good cop in Cedartown. He's a guy named Walter McKinley. The newspapers nicknamed him 'Bear' because of his size"

"Newspapers?"

"He was a good Toronto cop who exposed some corruption in the force. The newspapers loved him, the police force didn't. When it looked as though he was going to be kicked off the force, I suggested to the Chief," she gave him a sidelong glance and a shrug, "a friend of the house! That he be sent to Cedartown. He went along with it."

George raised an eyebrow, shook his head and smiled before giving his trying friend a final hug and kiss.

"Cedartown next, soldier!" The conductor shook him awake. Still woozy he grabbed his rucksack and staggered to the door. It was late and the sky was country black: not a hope of getting to the island tonight. He'd probably have to hot foot it into town and get a room at the Cedartown hotel, such as it was. He swayed as the train whistled, slowed, and then screeched to a stop. One light on the station's overhang emitted a sad cone of illumination and occupying every inch of it was John Nicholson.

George felt his smile reach right down to his toes. "John, you handsome S.O.B., how did you know I was arriving today?" He punched him on the arm and shook his hand vigorously.

John gave him an uninhibited hug. "Knew it would be soon so I came every night."

"Every night? For how long?"

"Don't know. A few weeks." He stood back and tilted his head. "You sound funny."

"Shrapnel. Doctors had to go deep to pick out all the bits. It's not going to get any better than this, cousin."

John, took his rucksack and put his muscular arm around his friend's shoulder. "Don't worry partner, I'll be your voice."

And he will be, which was fair; it evened the balance a touch.

They climbed into John's truck and George asked, "Any way we can get to the island tonight?"

"Sure is! I got it all organized."

"You've got a boat?"

"Yup." He turned to George with a pleased little boy smile.

"Whose?"

Still grinning, John shook his head and stared ahead,

As they drove through town and over the bridge of the Castor River, George said, "Remember the day we tossed a stick over the railing to see what happened to it as it twisted and tumbled through the falls?

"You and Cass were probably eight and I was six." John laughed.

"We wanted to know if the falls had treated Dan the Chinaman the same way when he jumped."

"And then we went and put our noses against the window of Dan's café and were convinced we could see Dan's ghost, dressed in a long Chinese gown, wandering around in the back of the café."

"Cass would have none of it! She stamped her foot, furious at us that we believed we saw anything."

They laughed at the memory, and were quiet thinking about it.

"You didn't really see his ghost, did you?" John asked.

"You didn't?" George asked.

"No, and I remember it worried me a whole lot."

George laid his head back and smiled at the memory. "It's good to be home." He felt as though all the muscles throughout his body had released. Damn! He hadn't realized he'd been stretched so tight for so long.

When they arrived at the top of the hill looking down, he saw, tied up to, and occupying the whole south side of the harbour, was the Wawanesa –his Wawanesa. "Whoa!! I left it in dry dock!" He stared at the newly painted apparition. "How did you do it?"

"When I was released, I got it out and have worked on it ever since. Sanded, plugged and painted. Looks good, don't it?" His expression turned serious, "Thought we could maybe be partners."

George shook his head smiling. "It looks better than good, partner, it looks beautiful." It was just a wooden passenger boat with a large empty hull for storage, an elevated enclosure with a windshield in front of the steering wheel and open benches in the back. Not much, but his.

They parked the car and climbed in. "You want to drive her?" John asked.

"No cousin, you drive." He rubbed his hands along the edges, greeting his old friend. "I want soak it all up"

After the boat had hummed out of the harbour and, as soon as they hit the blue-black water, daughter of the night sky, John pushed the throttle. Leaning his elbows on the side George watched stars' reflections dance on the gentle ripples, and turned his face to the breeze. "Hello Wind," he whispered.

"Did you see Cass in Toronto?" John called over his shoulder.

"Of course."

"How is she?"

"Still got that 'don't-you-dare look' that teases the hell out of her customers."

"You still love her?"

"Can't help it,"

"Too bad."

In the middle of the lake, George put his hand to his neck and croaked as loud as he could over the noise of the engine, "Why don't we stop for a while?" Damn, it hurt! He'll have to touch for attention. He wondered how people would react to George Brown touching everyone he comes upon.

John turned the engine off and moved back to sit beside him. They were silent for a while letting the boat be master of its own whims. They were at least a mile out from Cedartown and more than that from the island. They, the boat, and the lake were one. The gentle floating of the big weight was lighter than a lullaby.

"Why do you think Cass does what she does?"

John's question yanked him back, He supposed it couldn't last forever but the feeling was so damned good it hurt to come back. "I don't know. Could be many things." When they were no more than young teenagers and he had been angry with her for her promiscuity, she'd stomped her foot and said, "Men will do anything for a bit of sex, so why shouldn't I? Anyway, It's fun." But he didn't want to talk about Cass. It hurt too much.

"What about you, John, Was it bad in prison?"

John shook his head slowly and looked down at the boat's bottom.

He scraped a foot back and forth along the moistened slats. "It was like being an animal in a cage but worse because we couldn't wag our tails or bark. With everyone in the same stripes, forced to march in a straight line and told when they could eat and sleep, I was close to exploding. I tell you cousin, I just made it."

"It wasn't one of your smartest moves, cousin."

"I thought, since the owner wanted it, it would be ok." He smiled, "Guess I was wrong."

George stared up at the stars. "Funny, isn't it? They put men in prison for committing a crime, and in the army, they put men in identical uniforms, make them march in a straight line, tell them when they can eat and sleep and they do it all to make them numb enough to kill." For a while they shared a silence weighted with memories. Finally, George pushed himself to his feet and patted John on the back. "You can forget prison, and I'll forget war. It's a new day, partner. You can be my voice and I'll keep you in tow."

"It made a bad scrape in my memory, sure hope it heals over. But we won't change our old ways?"

"Nope, we'll have our fun and skirt the law but not break it, at least not much. Now get the boat going, I'm anxious to get home.

The island harbour hadn't changed in five years. No more than piled railway ties, longer on the sides and shorter at the top of the squared 'U' where the hull of his grandad's original Wawanesa had been dug into the ground and stood erect, changed into a rustic office. He felt the urge to crawl out and kiss the earth but, after a peek at John, chose to kiss his hands and rub them on the earth of his home, his home, finally.

"You gotta be real tired. Go on up to your house. I'll put the boat to bed, partner."

Before starting up the path George turned to look back at Big John, whose blond hair was flopping forward as he secured the boat's ropes on the imbedded rings."

"A perfect homecoming partner. Thank you."

Looking pleased, John brushed aside his hair and waved away his thanks. "Aw, it was nothing."

He followed the thyme-laden path, through the woods to the house built by his grandfather, added to by his father. Nothing grand, it was a weathered wood square with a lower-roofed addition on the north side and a screened-in porch covering the bigger square. He could feel the welcome in this place full of memories that had been waiting for him for five years. It had obviously been cleaned from top to bottom—John, he was sure, had done it. He wandered from room to room touching, smelling, and smiling.

A loon's haunting cry echoing across the lake woke him early and smiling. He was home. He put his hands behind his head and stared out the window at daylight creeping across the water. Home: it was a word that wanted some thought. Before leaving it never crossed his mind to need attention; it was a permanent thing like water and wind and sky, but now, having been away from it for five years he guessed it was a word more like 'breath' or 'blood flow'. He threw his feet out of bed, shook his head, and stretched with pleasure.

Still naked, he gathered up his uniform and rucksack, went downstairs, and in the kitchen riffled around in the cupboards until he found some matches that, surprisingly, still worked. With his load, he started down the path smiling as he inhaled the remembered fragrance of the cedar path, and picked up driftwood on his way. At the lake, he built a substantial bonfire. Once the flames were crackling, in went the rucksack, and then the pants. He tore the medals off the jacket and with a final fling slammed it into the fire, as well. He jiggled the medals in his hand, then threw them one by one into the shadow in the woods; they didn't deserve the lake. As the ashes blew out over the water. He watched Wind take them away from the island.

That done, he dived in Lake, swam out and under and out again, and every time he came up for air he couldn't hold back a belly laugh of pleasure.

CHAPTER 2

"What's the plan?" John asked as they pulled into the harbour of Cedartown.

"I'm going to introduce myself to the new cop in town."

"What do you want to do that for?"

"Best to keep the law friendly."

"I s'pose, but count me out on that visit. I'll go and see Annette."

"Is she your latest?"

"She's special, George."

"As I remember, they've all been special for you, cousin."

John brushed his hand through his fair hair and tilted his head with an innocent look not sure how to answer.

"First we have to have coffee at The Little Brown Jug."

From behind the counter Elsa looked up and smiled. "George! It's wonderful to see you! When did you get home?"

"Just yesterday, Beautiful Elsa. You know I wouldn't wait a dog's moment before coming to see you." He sat down on one of the stools of the curved bar surrounding Elsa. John sat down beside him.

Elsa immediately stopped what she was doing and leaned over the counter to give him a hug. "I heard you were injured, but didn't know how."

"Shrapnel," he repeated yet again.

She backed away to get a better view of him. "Not so bad to get out of that mess with just a whisper."

"And he's got me to talk loud for him," John added.

"From now on we'll call you 'Speaker'," Arthur Rhodes called from the end of the counter, where he was perched on a stool with his little legs dangling in the air and a large camera on the seat beside him. "And George, will be 'Whispering George'! Now, I won't be the only one with a nickname!" Rhodes, the steeplechase jockey, caught doctoring an opposition horse, had retired to Cedartown where he had immediately been given the moniker 'Jumper', He did not accept it with humour.

"Bound to happen," George laughed. He looked around soaking up another symbol of home. The place hadn't changed a bit. The red leather cushions in the booths had, for more years than he could count, suffered the attention of squirming children, pubescent teenagers, unwashed bums, solid farmers and disapproving spinsters. "The place hasn't changed at all! He picked up the menu and laughed, "Not even the menu!"

Elsa laughed. "I tried to change it but the customers wouldn't have it. They like the fact they know the choices one through ten by memory."

George chuckled. "I remember the whole damn thing, too, even that the 'Cedartown Special' is made up of leftovers disguised with hot pepper in the sauce."

She shrugged her shoulders. "And it sells equally well."

"It's my favourite," John added.

Elsa served them each coffee, to which John, now Speaker, surreptitiously added a healthy glug of hooch, and as they sipped they watched Elsa go about her work, with the efficiency of experience.

The door opened and George looked over his shoulder to see Malcolm Fraser come in. Should he stand up? No, damn it, that time is finished. "Captain," he acknowledged over his cup of coffee. "Down from the city for the season?"

"Good to see you home, George, you've had a long haul." He sat down on the stool next to him. George could smell whisky on his breath. "I'm retired, so no more 'Captain'," he pleaded. "Malcolm or Fraser but not 'Captain'.

That would be a bit tough. After all, the man was a wealthy Torontonian who'd had a cottage in Cedartown forever. He used to hire George to take him and his friends hunting and fishing in the good rivers. He was, "Sir" in those days so it would probably work best still.

"Mr. Fraser has been here all year," Elsa said as she poured the Captain a cup of coffee.

"Needed a rest," Malcolm Fraser smiled.

Of course, he did. George had been with him through the worst of it, but he didn't have to return to Toronto and explain to the mothers how their sons had been murdered on the Moro River. It had been a massacre. Those who survived bullets were gnawed to death by Doberman Pincers. It was hell for him and the other survivors but it must be a mind-burning disaster for Captain Fraser.

"Are you up for a trip to my duck pond?" the Captain nervously flicked his hand back and forth across his ear as he spoke.

"Thanks, but not yet," George's voice cracked as he spoke. "Have to settle in first."

The Captain pushed himself away from the counter, "Just let me know. I have a new Labrador retriever, great dog, but not much use." He laughed, "Has a soft bite, but quakes at the sound of a gun."

George understood the dog—surprised the Captain didn't. He watched the man, who had held them together through the worst of it, as he walked to the door. He was tall, thin and straight and carried himself with an unconscious dignity. Memories sewed up tight in his innards.

When Elsa returned to them George whispered, "Thought I'd go over and meet the new cop. Do you know him well?"

"Very well. He's a good man, George."

Had George seen the colour rise on Elsa's cheeks?

"He's probably in his office now," she added.

George pushed himself off the stool. "I'll be off then." He smiled at Elsa. "It's good to be back Elsa, and especially good to find everything the same."

"I'll see you at 3.00," Speaker called after him.

George crossed the road and went into the town hall and the police office.

Clara Seaborne was still behind the secretary's desk typing away at her Underwood. How long had she worked there? It had to be twenty-five years. He bet that chair and the desk were her island.

Hands in pocket, head tilted shyly to the side, George croaked, "Clara My Friend."

She continued typing without looking up, but the smile on her face gave her away. "George Brown, back from away; home to put more grey in my hair."

George smiled. "A fine welcome home that is."

Clara Seaborne pushed her chair away from the desk and shook her head. "It's ridiculous to be pleased with your return, but I must confess it's wonderful to see your swarthy face." She stood up, put her hands on the back of her hips, thumbs forward, "But if you get up to your old shenanigans I might be less welcoming next time."

"C'mon Clara, I would never hurt a flea."

"That's the damned truth about you, mister. You seem able to skirt the law without doing so."

"How is Michael?" Clara had not had children of her own, which had not surprised George as she was so skeletal her bones probably would not have had the strength to carry a child. But she and her husband Andrew made up for it by taking in foster children to live with them on the farm. They came and went, but Michael remained and the couple adopted him.

"Growing." She smiled and shook her head. "He's quite human now, actually capable of adult conversation."

"Let me guess, he must be eighteen now."

"He is and with all the itches that accompany the age." She spoke with severity but love seeped through.

George shook his head and croaked, "He's galloped through five years without me. But I'm here now, Clara. I could have him help me on the island boat," he teased, "And with any other things that might come up."

"Not on your life, George! I haven't worked all these years to have him fall into the hands of a rogue like you!"

"C'mon Clara he'd love it." He was distracted by a familiar stench that permeated the room. "That's a smell I haven't forgotten! Frenchie's still around I detect!"

Clara looked over her shoulder as though she could see the cells behind the closed door. "Each time he spends the night after a drunken spree, we have to Javex the cell."

"He's still cleaning septic tanks then." He had his hand on his nose. "Anyway, I've come to meet the new cop."

Unable to stow her smile, Clara shook her head, "Go on in."

The man called 'Bear', evoked a bear in size, but as he rose from his desk and walked over to shake George's hand his movements were very un-bear-like, silkier and light. He was young, but for reasons unknown to George, had left behind the arrogant mien that often accompanies men in their early thirties.

"I'm George Brown, just back, and thought I should introduce myself."

Bear shook his hand. "Cass told me all about you. I've been looking forward to meeting you." He stared at George. "Seems you're very special to her."

George nodded. "We grew up together on the island. "Cass mentioned you, but I didn't realize you were friends."

The cop's head tilted the tiniest bit to the left, which gave George the uncomfortable sensation that he was not being looked at straight on, but was rather seen from a distinct perspective. "We are, and she told me about the house on the island in case she ran into trouble."

"Which is sure to happen with the life that wench leads."

Bear steered George to the chair in front of his desk, walked over and closed the door then perched on the front of the desk facing George. "Cass came to me for help when some of her girls were being attacked on the street. The police reaction was that it served them right. Not mine." Bear smiled. "It caused a bit of a ruckus within the hierarchy of the force, when I arrested some prominent individuals who had been involved in the attacks. But Cass with her dubious connections saved my bacon."

"She would."

"We became friends, and last year, when I confided in her my suspicions of fraud in the force, she helped me expose it."

"Could be you were playing with fire. I hope to hell Cass's involvement isn't public knowledge."

"Nobody knows about Cass. But the higher-ups did know that I was the culprit and wanted to kick me off the force." He pushed himself away from the desk. "But, through her connections, Cass saved the day and weaseled me a job here in Cedartown. So here I am."

"It must have been tough for you to leave the city."

He smiled. "When I arrived, I thought that the people living in a town like this, one that didn't exactly promise the citizens a glowing future, would be backward and uninteresting, and I was angry as hell and feeling badly used." He crossed his arms and looked down at the floor then, without lifting his head sought George's eyes. "How was I to know that here in this faded place the people think longer and harder than any 'sophisticated' city slicker?"

"Probably because there's no more than a thousand people hereabouts." George croaked. "Surface conversations fast get to be boring and repetitive, so they get torn open and dug into."

"Um-hmm, Bear agreed. "These people have taught me to go slow and think hard, and I can tell you, George Brown, neither attribute was very popular in the city." He smiled, and lifted his head. "They thought they were going to ruin my life by demoting me to Cedartown. If they knew how much I'm enjoying it, they'd probably transfer me again."

George decided he liked the man, which could cause a few difficulties for himself and John, but make the teasing more tempting. They'd have to be careful. "Do you like to fish Officer McKinley."

"Bear, please. It's the only name I go by around here. And yes, I like to fish."

"Once I get settled we'll go. I'll show you some good spots for trolling. The shoals haven't moved in my absence."

Bear stood up and shook his hand. "Thanks, and count on me to help if any problem for Cass arises."

"I'll remember, and pray neither of us will ever be needed."

In the afternoon, before returning to the harbour, he went to the hardware store and ordered four eight foot by five foot mirrors delivered to the Wawanesa. He would need John's help with them. It would be next to impossible to explain his need, but he'd go along.

When John arrived at the boat and saw the four cardboard-wrapped boxes he climbed in the open back and stared at them. "What's this, then?

"Mirrors," George croaked.

"Mirrors? What do you need with so many huge mirrors? You're not beautiful enough to want to see so much of yourself, cousin."

"I'll explain when we get them up."

He had just started the engine when a face leaned over the windshield. "Before you leave could I talk to you for a minute, George?"

Surprised, he switched off the engine and climbed out. Other than surface salutations he had never spoken to Mrs. Fraser. She was the daughter of Cedartown's wealthiest merchant and had married The Captain and lived the greater part of their life in the city, but her father, a wise and clinging man had gifted the couple a large cottage as a wedding present, which succeeded in keeping the pair and their kids entwined in the family roots.

She walked down the edge of the harbour expecting him to follow. At the confluence of the Castor River and the harbour she stopped and turned to him. Clouds blocked the sun making it difficult to see her face. Her edges were soft, and her voice was gentle. "I think, if you explained to me what happened to Malcolm overseas, I could, perhaps help somehow."

What could he say? How could he explain that, over there, their early innocence was short-lived, that the bombing, the killing and above all, the fear, turned them into a lethal group bent on extermination? How could he say that as the paralysis wears off and the conscience functions once more, no soldier can escape the bad dreams and the drinking and so many other contrary behaviors?

He pawed the ground with his foot, and didn't look at her. "It's almost impossible to explain if you haven't been there. We've all come home different, but I think it was harder for The Captain because he was responsible for his battalion so he felt their deaths were his fault." He looked up at her, "But for him, I think the worst part was having to return to Toronto and explain to all the mothers of your friends how their sons had died."

She looked over his shoulder and said in a detached tone, "That was probably why he wanted to move to Cedartown.".

"Is there anything I can do to help?"

She blinked and smiled a wan smile. "He has trained his children to pour his drinks. Tess pours two ounces, John three, and little Essie is proud to fill his whole glass with rye."

"Can't you stop them or him?"

"If I try, my gentle husband becomes vicious, not physically, but verbally and with great talent." She put her hand on George's shoulder. "When Essie pours he becomes very emotional and I worry that he might do something to himself. If ever I send for you, could you please come quickly?"

"'Course I will." If I'm on the mainland,

She nodded her head and minced her lips with a look that suggested that that worry was taken care of. He rubbed his chin and shook his head as he watched her walk to her car. Explaining war was impossible, like grasping air.

Once back on the island, they carried the boxed mirrors up to George's house, unpacked them, and leaned them standing, against various pieces of furniture.

John stared at them in confusion. "Now what?"

"We empty everything out of the pantry and attach one of these babies to each of the four walls." John's unblinking stare suggested that his cousin had returned with a bit more damage than was known, and it well could be, because George needed the damn mirrors.

Once they had achieved their task they stood in the center of the cubicle and each turned in circles. John, now Speaker, scratched his head but remained mute trying to figure what was going on.

"This is exactly what I wanted cousin. Thank you for the help.

"O.K. Now tell me what you need this for."

"Here, I can look at myself from behind and from the sides and get to think about the things I don't see about myself." He turned John around and looked over his shoulder at the mirror. "You can't understand others until you understand yourself and the questions you haven't asked." And most important, here there is no shadow, but that's not to be talked about.

John stared at their combined reflection. "Mirror, mirror on the wall, who is the nuttiest of us all?"

George laughed and swatted him gently on the head. "You're probably right, and worse still I'm going to put an easy chair in the middle with a table of books beside me so I can do my reading and thinking here. It will be my secret den with only you knowing about it, if that's ok."

"Don't worry about that. I wouldn't want the world to know some of that shrapnel hit higher than your voice box!"

"Thanks partner."

Chapter 3

1950

In the damp shadows of hovering evergreens, George poured his raw whisky into bottles that he and John had collected at the dump. He'd washed them out in the lake, but their cleanliness was a mite questionable. There was something in the bible about pouring new wine in old bottles being a bad idea, but this was hooch not wine and it didn't matter to his customers, so what the hell.

He settled the bottles into a dozen different crates and after admiring his work, sat on the ground and leaned his back against a tree to wait for Speaker.

It had been a good year. He had settled in with less difficulty than expected, probably because of the strength of new and old friends: Speaker, Elsa, Bear (who had melded into Cedartown life with surprising ease), and most of all Cass who worried him continually but regularly assured him, to "Stop worrying Georgie, I'll get out in time."

Above him he watched a swallow dip and dive, and sail with the breeze, freer than even he was. A black crow dove into the trees 'caw-cawing' a screech not unlike his own voice. "We're both where we want to be, Crow," he whispered to the bird. "Neither of us is beautiful but we damn well own our lives." He scooped up some moist soil and massaged it through his fingers. Putting some to his nose, he inhaled the humus of Home. What more can a man want? All this and, thanks to his mirrored room, he can escape the shadow permitting him to think long and hard and read books, because all the beautiful letters present themselves effortlessly.

He stared at the results of his labours. It was a big job to turn rye into mash and from there, to wort, and then let it ferment in the still for seven days. It made a man feel accomplished, and its illegality added a tang to the flavor. Now, all he had to do was put it aboard the Wawanesa and take it to Cedartown.

Dead branches cracked in the woods. Speaker's arrival was never quiet: a result of his inability to look anywhere but straight ahead. George inhaled his final moment of peace and forced himself to his feet.

"All done?" Speaker interrupted his ruminating.

George blinked back to the real world and nodded down at the loaded crates. "All done. Now, have to get these babies to the boat."

"You mean I do." Speaker lifted one crate without difficulty, stuck it under one arm and gestured to George to place a second crate under the other arm.

"You sure you can carry two like that?'

Speaker rolled his eyes.

"Sorry! While you do that. I'll fire up the Wawanesa." He looked at the remaining crates and extracted two bottles to carry.

"Time is it?"

George ducked the branches Speaker had let whip back at him. "Coming on seven." He croaked

"It'll be dark by the time we get these loaded and head for the harbour."

"That's the plan."

"You think Bear McKinley knows what we're up to?"

"Most likely."

"Is he going to stop us?"

"I think not."

"Why wouldn't he?"

"He's selective with his use of authority." His voice cracked on the word 'selective'. "He's a good cop; we're damned lucky to have him."

"You mean because he's the first cop sent to Cedartown who wasn't 60 years old."

"I mean he's a man with spine. The son-of-bitches who run the city should have rewarded him for what he did. Instead they kicked him down here to Cedartown."

"We're in luck then."

"Our luck. His load."

By 9p.m. they were on their way. The night was clear. Stars danced light on the rippled water. The whispered tune of the Wawanesa's engine dissipated in the vastness of the open lake.

Half an hour later they pulled the big wooden passenger boat along the harbour edge, eating up all the space on the south side. With the rope in hand Speaker leapt out and tied it to one of the two anvils anchored into the cement harbour wall, then sprinted to the front to receive the second rope tossed out by George. That done, they sat themselves in the open back and awaited customers who dribbled in bit by bit, paid their money, and scurried out quickly.

"I hear the council is going to vote on whether to keep the town dry," one of the customers said.

"They will." George whispered.

"Why do you think that?"

"Most of them are Presbyterians," he answered. He took the man's money, and gave him two bottles.

"Well I think they should vote a few Catholics in to change the vote. I'm not sure how much longer my gut will be able to deal with your Screech."

"You don't have to buy it."

"And I wouldn't if I could get into the city and buy the good stuff."

"Hell, you couldn't afford it anyway."

They watched him walk off in a huff, climb into his dilapidated Ford truck and drive off.

"That's the last bottle." Speaker bent his head and climbed out from the cabin. "You can go back alone, George. I'm going to see Annette."

"Watch yourself cousin. We don't want any little Annettes getting in our way."

"Don't worry about me none, George." Speaker pounded his huge chest. "I got experience!"

George pulled bills from all his pockets and began to straighten the crumpled mass. "I seem to remember Luis Lacoste arriving on the island with a gun and a pregnant daughter."

"That's the experience!"

George laughed and handed the organized pile to his cousin. "Here, before you go, count the money. I want to sniff the air a while longer." He slouched back on the bench and stared up at the moon. "Almost full."

"Tomorrow." Speaker said between licks of the finger.

A bang from up the hill crashed through the silence—then another and another.

Speaker jumped, George froze. "What in Hell?"

"Those are rifle shots. Sounds like they're coming from up the hill. Best we have a look-see."

Speaker pocketed the cash and climbed out of the boat behind George.

"There he is." Speaker pointed at the shadowed figure staggering down the hill.

"It's Mike Mason."

"Poor bugger."

"We have to stop him!"

George grabbed Speaker's arm to hold him back. "Can't go straight at him. The man doesn't know what he's doing. He pointed to the right. You go from that side and I'll take the other."

"Mike," George tried to call and cursed his inability, to make noise. "You talk Speaker. Go gently," he rasped.

"Mike," Speaker took over. "What are you up to, Man?"

George slipped towards Mike from the side using the trees as protection but he could see he'd have to go out in the open before reaching him. Mike kept shooting. The harbour gas tank was within range.

"Fuck You, God!" Mason screamed as he shot in the air again and again. He was twirling and screaming and crying.

"It won't help Mike! Don't make it worse," Speaker yelled

"My Boy, my Davey, Davey!" he screamed.

"What's going on over there?" A voice yelled from the other side of the harbour.

"Damn it. It's that son-of–a bitch Colt Black." Speaker called.

"Ignore him. We have to get that rifle." George croaked from the shadows. "I'll try to get behind him." He didn't know if Speaker could hear, but he'd know without words. Remaining in among the trees meant the route was more circuitous but he was getting close. Mike was still babbling and rubber-legging it down to the harbour but hadn't let off another shot. Maybe he had no bullets left. Speaker was crooning at him with a silk-smooth voice but Colt Black's yells screeching across the water were drowning him out.

"Can't you idiots do something about the stupid bastard?" He screamed from across the harbour. "Grab the son-of-a-bitch and we'll have the cop throw the bugger in jail!"

George was almost there; almost within reach when Mike Mason lifted his gun and shot at the voice. George grabbed him from behind, released the gun from flaccid hands and hugged the sobbing man.

Speaker came up, picked up the rifle, and patted Mike Mason on the back.

"It's alright," George whispered. "It's alright."

"Maybe not," Speaker frowned and stared across the harbour. "I think Colt Black's been hit."

Mike Mason collapsed to his knees, put his hands over his face and screamed.

"Oh Christ! Take the dingy across and check on Colt." George rasped. "And go into his house and phone Bear. I'll stay with Mike." He put his arm around Mike's shoulders and encouraged him to his feet. "Come and sit in the Wawanesa while we wait for Bear." He steered him to the boat and into the open back where he sat him on the bench that surrounded the inner perimeter and from underneath pulled out a bottle. "This will quiet you down."

CHAPTER 4

At The Little Brown Jug, George and Speaker sipped their morning coffee. "If you're planning to add some hooch you'd better do it fast," George whispered to Speaker. "Bear is waiting to come in." They both looked surreptitiously over their shoulders and saw the policeman leaning over the wheel of his car pretending to look elsewhere.

Bear loped in, put his hat on the counter and chose a stool facing them. Elsa smiled at him and brought his coffee. "Morning, Bear." She poured the dark liquid into his cup and lightly slid her fingers over the back of his hand.

"Morning Elsa." He nodded at George and Speaker. "Gentlemen."

"Did you hear that George? We're 'Gentlemen!"

"I like it," George mumbled

"I meant it as two words." Bear smiled at them.

"What does that mean" Speaker looked confused.

"Don't worry about it, cousin, it's a compliment: misplaced but nice."

Speaker frowned and returned to his coffee. "What happened down at the harbour?" Elsa asked. "I want to hear it all. Give me a minute." She quickly poured coffee for other customers, popped toast in the toaster and broke eggs on to the grill.

They waited in silence.

When she returned, she put her elbows on the counter, and leaned in. Her breasts gently nudged the apron that covered them. "What happened down at the harbour last night?"

"How did you hear about it?" Bear asked

"Mira."

"That damned telephone operator listens in to all the calls."

"She's the Mistress of our party lines."

"George and Speaker can tell it best, they were there."

George took a sip of his coffee. "We'd just pulled in the Wawanesa when we heard a rifle being fired" his voice began to weaken. "You tell it Speaker."

Speaker poured the cooled coffee from his saucer back into his cup. "Mike Mason was rubber legging it down the hill - -" he retold the whole episode.

"Poor Mike Mason," Elsa shook her head. "He's not been the same since their little boy has been fighting for breath in an iron lung."

"At least he shot the worst son-of-a bitch to ever reside in this town." George growled, and then felt guilty, but just a little.

"Is Colt dead?"

"No. They called from the hospital an hour ago," Bear told them. "The bullet ticked his brain and he's in serious condition." He sipped his coffee. "Mike will be sent to Kingston Penitentiary for a good long time."

Elsa collected their coffee cups. "We'll have to think of some way to help Alice Mason. She'll be desperate for money."

"I knew he was drinking too much," Bear grimaced, "Should have kept a closer eye on him." He rubbed his forehead. "Thing is, he didn't start drinking until little Danny became paralyzed and before now, he never hurt anybody but himself. Still, I feel responsible."

"None of that," Elsa insisted. "Let's concentrate on what we can do for Alice."

Everyone silently mulled over possibilities of aid. George leaned into Speaker's ear and whispered for an attention-getting length of time. Speaker raised his eyebrows, and nodded continuously until George finished. "Great idea cousin!"

"What?" Bear asked.

Speaker smiled. "Just somethin' we're considering."

"Do you want to share your idea? I might be able to help."

"Sorry, Bear, this one's private," George answered.

Bear leaned in towards them resting on his elbows. "A private idea shared by you two raises hackles, my friends. Your history precedes you."

"C'mon, Bear, we've never hurt anyone."

"True, but I suspect you dance on the verge of criminality."

"Can't help it, Bear, it keeps the twitch in our smiles!" George said and Speaker nodded, but with a frown, seemingly unsure of what George meant.

Elsa, Bear, Speaker and George continued to throw out ideas when something out the window seemed to catch Bear's attention and his return to the conversation drifted. The Captain's daughter, Tess Fraser, was bounding across the street, heading in their direction. George looked back at Bear who grimaced and quickly turned back to his coffee before the girl-child, with colt-thin legs, and little breasts opened the door.

Careful Bear, there's danger there. He watched Elsa refill Bear's cup and look at him and then at Tess who had plunked herself down on the stool next to Bear.

Tess knocked affectionately against Bear's shoulder causing him to frown and jerk away.

"Welcome home, Tess," Elsa said, still looking back and forth between the two of them. "It must be good to be back."

"Hi Elsa, may I have a coke please? And yes, I'm home for the summer." She leaned into Bear. "I got the job as Red Cross swimming instructor down at the pier so we'll see a lot of each other Mr. Walter Bear McKinley."

George watched over the top of his coffee cup.

Tess smiled her thanks to Elsa when the coke arrived and sipped from the straw while staring up at Bear through long dark lashes.

Bear got up to leave and Elsa followed him to the door. "I'll close at eight o'clock. Come back when you can." Although she had whispered, and George had not turned his head he knew what she said and was pleased for them both. Before Bear could open the door Arnold 'Jumper' Rhode arrived carrying a camera, which was disproportionately large on his short frame. "I'm glad I caught you, Bear. "I need information about the shooting, for the Cedartown Express." He blocked Bear's exit.

There was a streak of slime in the man's curiosity, no question. Nothing pleased Jumper more than to unveil secrets that damaged the reputations of good men and women.

"Mason has been arrested, and Colt Black is in the hospital in serious condition. That's all I can say for the moment." Bear replied stiffly.

"What initiated the scuffle? Was Mason drunk? What are the charges against him? Will Black survive?" He held his camera to his eye and flashed a photo of Bear.

"I've said all I'm going to say." There was acid in the policeman's response. Bear, too, it seemed, didn't like the sarcastic little pipsqueak.

As soon as Bear was gone Tess also got up to leave and on her way out called back to George, "Mom says to tell you Essie poured."

George put his cup down quickly and nudged Speaker. "Let's go."

As they were leaving Elsa called after them, "Any ideas how we can raise money for Alice, Boys?"

"We'll think on it," George answered from the opened door. "Right now we'd best go see the Captain."

Speaker got behind the wheel. "First to Joe McPhee's to get him to dig out his pipes." George whispered.

"Pipes?"

"His bagpipes. We'll take him over to the Captain and have him march back and forth on the lawn playing those pipes of misery."

"You don't like them?"

"Not one damned bit. They do nothing but spout memories of war."

"But the Captain does."

"Yup, they give him permission to cry."

With a confused frown on his face Speaker drove on facing ahead without saying another word.

With Joe and his bagpipes in the backseat, they drove to The Captain's large house overlooking the lake.

"You two wait in the car for about 5 minutes" George ordered, "Then, Joe, start marching back and forth at the front of the house with your pipes playing like Billie-be-damned.

Joe McPhee nodded, too busy mouthing his pipes to answer.

As George headed towards the house he was stopped by Young Essie's call. "Mr. George, Look at me!"

The child was hanging upside down on a trapeze her little dress hanging over her face leaving only her sweet underpants visible. "I'm very impressed Essie. I certainly couldn't do that."

"It's a half 'skin the cat'!"

"A half skin the cat? and what if you turned the whole way?"

"That would be a whole 'skin the cat', silly!"

George crouched down on the ground so he could look up at her little face through the overturned dress. "And would you tell me how you knew it was me, when your dress is covering your face."

"Your shoes, of course."

George looked down at his shoes. "My shoes?"

"Yes, silly, you're the only man in Cedartown who wears Indian moccasins."

"You are a very smart young lady, Essie."

"Thank you! Mr. Jumper says that too. He's going to put my picture in the Express one of these days, but not any of the pictures he took when I was upside down."

"I should think not!" George wasn't sure he liked that. "Where did you do your 'skin the cat' for him?"

"In the park at the lake." She twisted to a full 'skin the cat' and landed on her feet and swept at her dress, "He's always there taking pictures of the kids."

He patted her on the head, "Best you save your 'half skin the cat' for at home."

En route around to the back of the house that had a screened in porch overlooking the lake he saw Mrs. Fraser standing in the middle of her garden holding a large bouquet of flowers. She looked unsure as to where to step next. "Good morning Mrs. Fraser."

"Thank you for coming, George."

He went over to the round, pink-cheeked woman, and leaned into her bouquet for a whiff, before answering. "Of course." He stood up and looked towards the lake. "Where is he?"

"There on the porch," she indicated with the bouquet.

He looked over. The Captain was staring out at the lake tilted back in his chair with his feet up on the sill of the screened porch, and a drink in his hand. George nodded at Mrs. Fraser and headed in that direction. What was it about The Captain that made him think 'Old World'? He sure as hell didn't dress the part, and swore too much to sound sophisticated—might be the way he held his head erect on his shoulders, or maybe his long fingers that had never seen manual labour, but probably it was mostly his extreme good manners. He mounted the stairs. "Captain!"

"George, my boy," He didn't look up but waved his hand at the table holding a bottle of Seagram's Rye and a brass jug that had seen better days. "Get yourself a glass from the kitchen."

He didn't want a drink and decided to forgo any water when he saw the inside of the brass jug had a green tint.

"The Legion want me to march with them wearing all my medals." He swatted his ear. "I told them it was the last god-damned thing I would ever consider doing." He laughed. "I'm sure they thought I was above marching in little old Cedartown." He took a big slug from the glass of dark brown liquid. "Brought it all back—the whole damned nightmare." He turned to George, "You know how it was." George nodded.

They sat in silence bonded by memories.

And then the pipes started with their lonely moan. The Captain took his feet down and sat forward, ignoring Mrs. Fraser as she passed through, hugging her bouquet in one arm and with her free hand dragging Essie, who obviously wanted to stay and hear the pipes.

The Captain turned to George with moistened eyes. "You did this?"

George nodded, "Thought it might help."

The Captain sank back in his chair. "Makes my toes open and shut—it does."

Mrs. Fraser wandered out with a magnificent arrangement in a large vase which she placed on the table with the scotch and brass jug and then returned to the kitchen.

George got up and quietly left The Captain to the music of the pipes and a momentary exhalation of disturbing thoughts.

Chapter 5

Bear tapped on the window of the Little Brown Jug and Elsa peaked over the 'closed' sign before opening the door and pulling him into a hug.

"I'm sorry I'm so late," Bear apologized. "Busy night. Frenchie was drunk as usual, a fight broke out at The Dance Hall, and there were some strangers in town whom I needed to keep an eye on." He kissed her neck. "But nothing serious."

"It gave me time to clean up." She took him by the hand and they went behind the counter where there was a bottle of good rye hidden in a lower cupboard. Bear pulled out two glasses from the shelf and she unscrewed the top.

"Could be we're breaking the law serving alcohol in a restaurant. Especially illegal alcohol."

"Illegal only in Cedartown, and it's my restaurant and it's closed so now it's just my home." She filled both glasses; they clinked and sipped looking each other in the eye, both aware that the drink was a comfortable prequel to a pleasurable evening.

"You love this place, don't you?"

"I do," she agreed, "But even more, I love the people!"

He put his arm over her shoulder. "All of whom have special stories," he laughed, "And you're recording each one."

"Not each one; there are some that are too outrageous to be believable, and others so dull it would take genius to bring them to life on paper, but there's certainly lots of fodder." They leaned their elbows on the counter and stared out at the restaurant finishing their rye in silence, and then put their glasses in the sink and went slowly up the stairs to her apartment above the restaurant.

Their lovemaking was slow and smooth: comfortable and easy.

As she lay tucked in the crux of his arm, both stared up at the ceiling, each in their own world. Perhaps they slept. Bear was not sure.

"What are we going to do to help Alice Mason?" Elsa mumbled.

"We're going to get the Legion to donate the take from the Summer Square Dance. If Malcolm asks them they won't say no. He's something of a war hero to them."

"Good idea." She tilted her head up and stroked his chest. "You'd best steer clear of Young Tess, Bear. She's against the law, and she's after you."

"I know." If he said more he'd give himself away.

Elsa flopped her head back down. "I remember when I was fifteen: it was a time when curiosity and hormones were in a perpetual battle, making me bitchy and rebellious."

"And did you satisfy your curiosity?" He shouldn't have asked. Not when he was thinking of Tess.

She laughed. "No, I moped, was rude to my parents and ignored my schoolwork."

She rolled on top of him. "Let's try it like this."

He lifted her from under the arms, placed her perfectly, and they were off again, flying to oblivion.

Elsa shook his shoulder. "It's 4a.m. You said to waken you."

"Mm-mm." He pulled her into a hug. "I'd better get out of here while it's still dark, before the whole town knows that the local cop is sleeping with the most desirable woman in Cedartown."

"The whole town probably knows already." Her muffled response blew air on his chest. She tilted her head. "Will you stay in Cedartown, Bear?"

He kissed the top of her head. "Is that an Elsa MacTier prerequisite for a lasting relationship?"

"I'm afraid so." She sat up and hugged her knees, causing the sheet to fall away from breasts that were neither small nor large but round and golden and oh, so tempting. "When I went away to college I felt

I was suffocating the whole time. It's a physical thing. Only here at home can I breathe freely. Don't ask me to explain it because I don't understand it myself."

"Cedartown is lucky to be able to keep you in its clutches."

"I'm not the only one."

"I've noticed."

"We seem to need to be surrounded by everything that's familiar, and the minute we step away from our bubble we fear we're walking out of the electricity of life." She pushed the sheet aside and got up. "It's all unconscious with most but with me, it has a physical corollary. Away from Cedartown I feel ill."

He followed her naked body as she wandered to the kitchen. Such perfection! Narrow shoulders and flared hips and a waist around which his big hands almost met. Elsa was a polished work of art.

"But you haven't answered my question." Elsa called.

"Will I stay in Cedartown? I don't know." He stepped into his pants. "I'm not a very good cop. For me, it's tough to stick to the 'letter of the law' written by stodgy men dressed in legal robes who have never dipped the toes of their shiny shoes into the dirt of humanity."

Naked but for an apron, she brought him a cup of coffee. "Goodness! You sound angry."

"I suppose I am. The law lags. It doesn't sympathise with a girl who has to prostitute herself to feed her child, a man who drinks dangerously to drown the misery of the loss of his wife, or a wife who runs away with her children to avoid further beatings. Not to mention the enjoyment I get out of Speaker and George's nefarious undertakings."

"But without the law there would be chaos."

"Of course, you're right. But I find it too damned dictatorial!" He pulled on his pants and finished dressing.

She put her arms around him. "I know what you're saying, Bear, but I hope you don't go. You're a good man, and a good cop, and Cedartown loves you."

"We'll see." He started for the door.

Chapter 6

Driving down towards the harbour George was careful to avoid three kids pushing their bikes up the hill before mounting them. In high summer the place would be full of laughing children in bathing suits carrying towels around their necks, but in the chill of late May, the place was almost deserted.

Bear was parked in his cruiser across from the long landing area, where the Wawanesa was docked. He waited for George at the harbour's edge. "Can you come up to my boathouse for a minute?"

George's heart thumped. "Is it Cass?"

Bear put a consoling arm on his shoulder. "She's fine. She sent some papers for you to see."

George didn't understand. "Why not send them to me?"

"It's not that. She sent a whole package of papers for me as well, and some of the things you have to sign need a witness."

Together they walked towards the path that gave access to the row of dilapidated boathouses that lined the harbour. The first boathouse in the row belonged to Jack Winston who did a good business on the harbour side with a gas tank at the harbour's edge and a ramp at the back for repairing boats. Facing the park side, he had a booth which, in summer, was always busy because he staffed it with well-endowed young girls who served dressed only in their bathing suits. Now, the place looked forlorn with the booth window shuttered and the wind blowing scraps of paper across the pebbled area in front.

The park across from the string of boathouses was empty. The swing sets squeaked in the breeze and the ten doors of peeling green paint that lined the long low building of changing rooms, hung open. Beyond the row of boathouses was a long pier jutting out into the lake.

"Your family has been here for generations," Bear said. "Do you know when the pier was built?"

"Don't really know. It's been here all my life and I'm thirty-five."

"Whoever was responsible gave the town a source that doesn't exist anywhere else on the eastern shore."

George stared out at the long familiar pier which was so much part of his existence he barely noticed it and looked at it through Bear's eyes: horizontal bars of tubed black railings guarded the harbour side; three bars spaced widely—the lowest serving as a good footrest for fishermen, the second, preventing disastrous falls into the dense brown water of the harbour and the top railing accommodating the leaning elbows of dreamers.

On the lake side of the long pier huge rocks had been dumped haphazardly down from the cement walkway to create a gradual decent to the water, and at a hundred, and one hundred and ninety yards, were two cemented platforms from which the kids could swim. He could see the rippled sandy bottom through the crystal-clear water on the swimming side—a harsh contrast from the muddied water of the harbour. When overseas, George remembered every inch, every colour and every smell on the island, why not this? Strange.

Bear's boathouse, in the middle of the row, was in better shape than the other half dozen. "You've done a good job on the place. It didn't look different from any of the others before I went away."

"I worked hard on it. Painted it inside and out, and in the upstairs living area replaced windows, varnished the floors, and refitted the kitchen."

On ground level where they entered, the boathouse slip had a boat with a 50 horsepower Evinrude and on the walls surrounding the slip all the accoutrements of water life: ropes, life preservers, oars, water skis, and fishing rods, neatly stored on hooks or behind wooden supports. George was impressed with the meticulous organization of things.

"I'm pleased with the result," George smiled. He liked to hear the modest pride in Bear's voice.

Upstairs there was a small bedroom on the side with a bed made tighter than army style and the rest was one large, spotless room with a kitchen with shining counters at one end and doors opening on to a balcony overlooking the harbour at the other. The place was so clean he bet you could eat off the floor.

"A beer?"

"Thanks." A better offer than his hooch. He wondered if Bear had ever tasted it. "What's that supposed to be?" George pointed at an unframed painting tacked to the wall.

Bear handed him his beer. "I'm embarrassed to tell you," he laughed. "It's a portrait of me!"

"You?"

"It was explained to me that the huge, curved yellow lines are my outline, the small vibrant green dashes are my laughter, which, I was insulted to be told, is rare, and the eyes are the way I always see things tinged with a shade of grey."

"And the red circles?"

He blushed. "My cheeks when I'm angry."

"And who, may I ask created this wonderful work of art?"

"Young Tess, The Captain's daughter.

Of course!

What had Cass sent? It couldn't be good news

"I'll get the papers," Bear went to a kitchen drawer and took out a large manila envelope, which he carried to the table where he sat beside George and pulled out a stack of legal-looking papers. "These top ones are for you. Cass's will and her power of attorney. If you sign them, I'll witness them here."

George didn't want them. Especially her will. He didn't want anything that suggested danger to Cass. She worried him every moment of the day. He cleared his throat to fight the emotion in his voice. "And those other papers?" He pointed to handwritten notes.

"All sorts of information about corruption and bribes and even murder. She wants me to put them away in a safe place, just in case."

"Just in case! What a god-awful expression. It fills every pocket with a weight of worry."

Bear nodded and thrust his hand through his thick mop. "I don't want them. I don't want what they say and I definitely don't want the suggestion something might happen to Cass."

"No more than I want these."

"Shows how much she loves you, though."

"If it does, it's a pretty unbalanced love. It's a cart filled with friendship, memories, caring and yes, damn it, love, but Cass is forever adding to the weight or throwing something off. Either way it makes the cart tilt and I'm worried that one of these days it might spill its contents." George pushed himself away from the table. "I need to walk."

Bear lifted his bulk. "I'll join you if you don't mind."

They walked along the pier, lifting their faces to the refreshing wind. Wipe my tears, Wind, before he sees them, George pleaded.

At the head of the pier they leaned on the wall and stared out at the huge lake. George shook his head in wonder. "Sometimes the lake's furious, sometimes so damned calm it seems to exhale silence." Without taking his eyes away from the water he asked Bear, "Are you happy being a cop?"

Bear pushed himself straight and laughed. "Not when I have to deal with the likes of you and Speaker." Then he became serious. "My problem is that I can see Mike Mason handcuffed and in tears and I know that beneath the man's drunken burst of anger there was a helplessness, an inability to save his son. That's the really, tough part of policing." He grimaced in anger. "Sympathy's possible, forgiveness, sadly not, and the law is my unappealing mistress, whom I ignore too much." He scratched the back of his head. "At least for the moment it's the job I have."

"For the moment?"

"We'll see" They started back towards the landing area.

To change the subject from the prerequisites of the law that could affect him personally, George croaked, "I'm guessing you and Elsa have a liking for each other."

Bear stopped. "It's tough. I'm in a battle with myself and my future, and Elsa will have none of it if I have to leave Cedartown." He inhaled in annoyance. "I don't understand why she insists on staying here."

"I do," George mumbled. "When I was overseas all I could think of was the smell of home in the wind and the feel of the island's moist black soil, and the memories that made me." With surprise in his voice he asked, "Don't you have memories of your childhood home?"

Bear answered with a half-smile. "Never really had one. My dad was in the army so my home was my family." He smiled an apology, "We moved so often my memories are more emotional than physical."

"Stick around, and you may begin to feel that Cedartown is home." He dragged his hand along the railing. "When that happens, you'll understand her better."

Half way down the pier, they stopped and leaning on the iron railing stared out at the harbour in silence. Below them motorboats that had seen better days passed, their bows tilted high and manned by men sitting in the back seats with one arm twisted behind to manipulate the protruding arm of their outboard motors. At the entrance of the harbour a speeding inboard reduced its speed so dramatically it created a wake and, with a teenager at the wheel it hummed towards Jack Winston's gas tank.

"I'd best grab a quick lunch and then get back to the office or Clara Seaborne will think I've gone AWOL," he laughed, "Which is something worth considering."

George left him at his boathouse and continued on to the Wawanesa.

Speaker was sitting in the back of the boat absorbing the sun and reading the Cedartown Express. George climbed in beside him and Speaker handed him the front page. "Jumper is at it again.

George sat beside him and read:

WHERE WAS BEAR McKINLEY?

On Thursday afternoon, Mike Mason went on a drunken spree down at the harbour. He shot his rifle off repeatedly, causing consternation amongst the helpless onlookers.

Only Colt Black was courageous enough to interfere by yelling from the opposite side of the harbour. Using flamboyant language, he demanded that Mike cease and desist immediately.

Mason aimed his wavering rifle at the harsh words and shot Colt Black in the head. The bullet skipped past most of the brain but doctors say recuperation will be long and difficult.

Our Cedartown police officer arrived in time to arrest Mike Mason but not in time to stop him from creating destructive havoc.

Mason's recent drunken sprees were well known in town. Perhaps Bear McKinley should have paid more attention.

George shook his head. "Poor Bear."

Chapter 7

George sat in his chair behind the table in the center of his mirrored room. He let out a big breath and stared at his reflection. Speaker's reaction to the room was completely logical. He had a hard time even explaining it to himself, just like he couldn't explain the pleasure it gave him to skirt the law a touch.

Here, relieved of the damned hovering shadow, that wanted to envelop him in the screeching terror of war, he could contemplate the silent mirror that threw his profile, the back of his head, parts of himself that he couldn't see but others could, right back at him. The reflections initiated a thought, which mirrored another thought and on and on in endless succession.

Eyes closed, Bear came to mind. The big man was too nice to be a cop, too gentle. If he wasn't careful he'd fall into the same emotional quagmire as The Captain. And he'd best be careful of that girl-child Tess Fraser. Did she know what she was doing? Probably not consciously, but she sure as hell had to sense the effect she had on the young cop. He remembered seeing her approach Bear down at the harbour. She was licking an ice cream cone, letting it dribble down her chin and eyeing Bear over the top. Even he could sense the electricity that swirled around the two of them. Too bad chastity belts were out of practice.

The Captain probably doesn't see his daughter as anything but a beautiful young creature whom he adores.

He worried over the Captain. His buried dramas were eating him up. How long would it be before the shadows engulfed him? Passion was such a damned all-consuming emotion!

Both men would do well with his mirrors.

If Cass were here she'd know how to speak to Young Tess. She'd always been able to see through people. "It's why I enjoy sleeping with them all Georgie. I see them at their weakest and then, away from sex, I can recognize the pout or the jittery eyes or the weak smile for what it is."

And this, she told him, when they were still teenagers. "But do you like doing it?" He had tried not to sound disgusted because he already loved her.

"I like the power it gives me, Georgie Boy," she'd answered, as she gave him a hug to soften the words. "But you're my man and will always be."

That was why he had refused to sleep with her even with her teasing, "C'mon Georgie, it's fun!" Even then, he knew her sex was never accompanied with respect and without respect love was mush.

There was something coming, though, he could feel it. The will and the power of attorney were frightening.

Damn! The weight of it all needed relief, if not outright laughter! At least a smile every now and then to lighten life's worries.

"George" Speaker's voice and knock brought him out of his reveries. "Hawker's here."

George groaned, not interested in disturbing his contemplation for the big man who was overseeing the building of Cass's house. The Canadien was completely devoted to Cass, George had to give him that, but he couldn't run a two-holed outhouse let alone the renovation of a whole house.

Spectacles still sitting on the top of his head, George opened the door a slit with the intention of slipping out and closing it behind him, but Hawker pushed him back in. "What you hide in here Mr. George?" He stepped into the middle of the room, stopped, did a full circle and said in awe, "Ta-ber-nacle!" He sat down in George's chair and stared at the various reflections. "This place, it is sinful, Monsieur George!"

"Sinful?"

"Oui! I think our God, he not want us to know ourselves like dis."

"Like what?" Speaker asked from the door.

"From de back and de front and de sides. Dis place, it don't leave room for him."

George's skin prickled. He wanted Hawker out of there. "Is there another problem?" He had had to take his boat around the southern tip at least once a week over the last year to ensure that Hawker was overseeing the workers, and to hand out pay. The progress was slow.

"That's why I come. The inside painters, they need pay. Maybe big pay 'cause they don't like my dogs."

"Let's go see what's going on."

The coastline surrounding Cass's property was rocky. You had to know, or be told, where to land which was a good protection. They drove around to the west side and pulled in at the recessed dock beside the painters' boat.

The house could be seen from the shore: handsome, but simple; barn wood sidings with light grey trim around the windows.

They walked up the path through the woods and found the two painters backed up on the steps leaning into the door and frozen in place by a pair of growling wolf-dogs.

"God-damn-it, call these creatures off! They won't even let me pee!"

"Why you not go in the house," Hawker asked as pulled the animals back.

"The door locked behind us!"

"De button on de lock. You must have pressed it."

One painter ran off into the woods opening his pants as he went. The other growled, "Open the damned door. We want to pick up our stuff and get the hell out of here." The other returned looking relieved but standing well away from the dogs. "We're leaving. It's not worth it."

George, tried not to laugh at the poor buggers. "C'mon boys, you're making twice as much as you would in Barrie."

The man who was preoccupied with his bladder answered, "But there we can be damn sure we won't be hospitalized either by dog bites or constipation!"

"That's if we don't drown in a storm on our way over here."

"I lock up the dogs," Hawker dragged them by the collar to his cabin in the back. "Big mistake!"

George negotiated an expensive agreement and left the grumbling men outside as he and Hawker went in to check on the progress.

One large room dominated the first floor. It had windows on all three sides, enabling Cass to see every direction but north where there was an unnavigable swamp. The room was open to a kitchen on the north side. Upstairs had another large room and two bedrooms off to the side. The big room had only a large desk and comfortable chair.

"Cass, she say when she come, she write a book."

Please no, Cass. Come and forget it all. Come and smile with me.

CHAPTER 8

"Shh!"

"I tripped, God damn it! Who can see in these woods? Shine the light over here."

"Jesus Christ, Speaker, don't you know how to whisper?"

"We can't all whisper like you, George. Hold the light still! It's weaving all over the place."

"It's you that's weaving, mister. Be careful, don't drop the spears!"

"I've got them, I've got them!"

"Why the hell do we have to do this in the dark?"

"Do you want to do it during the day and get caught? Anyway," George added, 'It's a warm-up for the rest of the night." He was feeling the twitch in his smile. They arrived at the bank on the water's edge. "Would you look at that? There must be a thousand of those shiny, pickerel backsides fighting their way upriver!"

"And ripe for the picking. No wonder it's against the law to spear them."

"Don't worry, it's not a law they pay much attention to. Here, Speaker, give me my spear. Let's get in there and catch ourselves some pickerel for dinner."

"There, George, there's a big one, get it!"

"Someone's coming. I can see the flashlight up at the road!"

"Into the bushes! And turn off that damned flashlight!"

"Can you see who it is?

"It's that twerp Jumper with his camera."

"Trying to expose someone for his newspaper, I'd bet."

"Or for a little blackmail."

"If we try to leave we'll make too much noise. We'd better lie low."

They climbed the bank and sneaked well back into the woods with the agility of Indians or experienced criminals. Lying on their backs, they listened as Jumper bashed his way through the bush: then there was silence.

"He's hiding," George whispered.

"Waiting to catch someone." Speaker hissed. He passed his mickey of hooch to his friend who took a slug.

"Odious prick!" George hissed.

"Good word, where'd you learn it?" Speaker whispered back.

"The Captain uses it."

"Of course."

"Good thing we did taking Joe McPhee over to Captain Malcolm's to play the bagpipes."

"Yup. Took a while but we left him better."

"Did ya see the tears rolling down his cheeks?"

"Those tears had memories. Good to get rid of them."

They lay on the ground and stared up at the stars keeping their ears attuned to the possibility of an upcoming drama. Suspect undertakings often necessitated extraordinary patience and George was proud that he and Speaker, with the help of a shared bottle of hooch, could, if necessary, remain there all night. It was a prerequisite for the undertaking of questionable activities and disturbing the laws of the land was very pleasurable. "Will we get enough money for Alice tonight?"

"Nope! We'll have to figure out how to get more

"I hear a car."

Speaker knelt and pushed aside some branches. "It's a provincial police car."

"Looking for the likes of us."

"I don't think so." Speaker nudged George with his foot. "You have to see this!"

On their knees the two watched a pair of provincial police dressed with waders slip their way down the bank aided by the spears they were carrying. "Are you sure we should be doing this, Chief?" The smaller one said and looked around nervously.

"We'll be in and out before anybody finds out. Just one fish each and then we go." He speared a large pickerel and held it up in the air with satisfaction.

And a camera flashed.

Jumper appeared at the edge of the creek. "An excellent photo for the next issue of the Cedartown Express, Gentlemen!"

"Son-of-a-bitch!" Speaker whispered

The Chief dropped the speared fish on the bank. "You wouldn't dare you little runt."

"Oh, but I would, Chief." He held his camera up and flashed it again, then slipped back into the woods.

The two policemen tried to go after him but their waders and the muddy bank held them back.

"We might as well keep our fish, Chief. They were expensive enough."

"Shut up Sargent."

"We'd better lie low until their car disappears." Speaker handed the mickey back to George and they lay down to contemplate the stars once more.

"That Jumper is a sneaky son-of-a-bitch."

"It seems the man gets pleasure out of hurting people."

'Not an ounce of goodness in the man."

Speaker whispered. "Must be because he's so short he can't even sniff a woman's navel"

Speaker got up on his knees. "He's gone."

"We'd better be sure. It would not be good to have him follow us."

"He's had his thrill for the night. He's probably in bed making love to his camera.

"Just in case, let's skip the fish and go the long way out of here to where the truck is hidden. We have more important things to do."

They moved the branches gently and wended their way out.

Speaker took the wheel. "Where will we do it?"

"Let's go to the 5th concession. That's where Bob McTavish's farm is. I never liked the tight assed, religious, son-of-a-bitch. Once heard him say that over on the island we make love to the sheep."

"Squire Dawson does."

"Can't count The Squire, he's not all there. He says it's lonely on his end of the island, and the sheep keep a man warm on a cold winter night."

"O.K. It's the 5th concession.

It was 2a.m. as they drove along the graveled road of the 5th concession. Speaker peered over the steering wheel and stared up at the sky. "Not much moon tonight."

"A good thing. Pull up here. It's as good as anywhere to start." George hissed.

They pulled the truck over into the ditch and from the rear removed straps, spiked shoes, and wire cutters. "We have to get these things back into the Hydro truck before morning." Speaker turned towards the telephone poles. "You take the first, third, fifth and on and I'll take the even numbers."

George nodded and they set to work in silence. They climbed and snipped, climbed and snipped all the way along the 5th concession road. At 4a.m. having collected their bounty, they wound it all up and placed it in the truck.

"You don't have to drive so slowly, it's the middle of the night, there's nobody around." Speaker insisted.

George ignored him. "Best be careful."

"We'd best go straight to Newmarket. Be there when the place opens." Speaker decided.

George was silent for a minute. "Bear will see the Island Boat parked in the harbour all night."

"Not much we can do about that."

"Maybe you should go to Newmarket and I'll take the boat to the island. That way we'd have an alibi."

"Good idea, but I don't want to drive through town with this load."

"That's true." George contemplated the alternatives. "Ah to hell with it, "We'll both go. We can think of something while we're driving."

"We could say we were at the whore house in Orville."

"He'd check that."

"Maybe we could stop there and have a visit with Zelda, she'd give us an alibi."

"That's a possibility."

Chapter 9

The phone rang in the outer office and after she hung up Clara came into the office. "You'd better get out to the 5th concession."

"What's happened?"

"All the copper wires have been stolen. Every farm is without phone, and Bob McTavish from Dunedin Farm is insisting you bring in the Provincials."

"How much does copper sell for?"

"I'd have to look it up; at a guess about 35 cents a pound, but the thief would get only half that." Clara surmised. "Why would anyone go to so much trouble? Think of the work involved in reconnoitering the location, finding equipment to be able to reach the telephone wires, and then undertaking the whole damned thing in the dark!"

"It's the freedom of the thing."

"Until they're caught," she replied.

In the flat lands surrounding Cedartown streams were lazy and the soil was dark and moist. Along the unpaved concession roads were field upon field of infant corn, or early wheat, and lining the fields were ditches full of weeds, mud, bull rushes, wild strawberries and the odd brave flower.

In the distance, Bear could see the Bell Telephone workers up two poles already replacing the stolen wires. His concentration was such that he almost ran over a partridge that had popped out of a ditch.

He pulled up next to Bob McTavish's truck. The farmer was leaning against his truck with arms crossed, staring straight ahead. He did not acknowledge Bear as he approached.

Bear went up to him, "Bob."

The farmer spit out a stream of tobacco and took off his hat revealing a dramatic demarcation line on his forehead between exposed and covered skin. He banged the hat on his knee. "No need for you, Bear, I've called the provincials."

"I'm sorry you felt you had to do that, Bob."

"They'll know better what to do."

"I think they'll tell you this is my territory." Bear turned away from him, stepped through the mud in the ditch and went speak to the foreman. "How long until the phones are reconnected?"

"Be done by tonight."

"Good, and thanks." He returned to his cruiser without acknowledging Bob. He'll drive straight to Newmarket to find out who is selling copper wire.

The dirt road necessitated a low speed but when he hit the highway he settled in to the rhythm of the long drive. It had been a good night with Elsa, and the promise of many more made him feel a deep satisfaction. Elsa was right about Young Tess. He should avoid her like the plague. Imagine a fifteen-year-old painting a head like that. He shook his head trying to rid himself of his untoward thoughts. She was fifteen years old and he was a good man. Please God let him remain so.

He was so deep in thought he got only a fleeting glimpse of the truck passing in the opposite direction. Could it be The Boys? Would they be the culprits? Of course, they could be, but why? They always have a reason even if their logic is a little lopsided. He'll check the traders in Newmarket but if any of them are buying stolen copper they'll not open up to him, he was sure.

When he gets back, he told himself, he must go and see Alice Mason.

The houses on the Mason's tree-lined street were quiet and solid, many with large, unused front porches. The Mason's home was no different in size and shape but its paint was peeling and it was next to the railway line, which caused it to shiver when a train screeched through.

Before he reached the front door, Alice Mason opened it. She looked wan and thin, and her smile seemed a great effort.

Bear took off his hat as he stepped through the door. "How's Young David, Alice?"

She sighed, and shook her head. 'Come and see for yourself."

Bear was taken aback to see George sitting at the head of the machine wiping the boy's head with a moist cloth. "You seem to be everywhere, George."

"Doing what little we can, Bear." He didn't look up from his task.

"Where's Speaker?"

"Fetching some supplies for Alice here. He'll be back soon."

Seeing his surprise Alice said, "George and Speaker have been very, very helpful."

'I'm sure they have." Of course, it was their truck he saw pass as he was driving to Newmarket.

The iron lung enclosed a long, flat bed with a cylindrical cover and took up most of the small room making the tiny head peeking out from the end appear even smaller. Beside the iron lung was a large pump that sucked and released in a loud, repetitive, hissing rhythm.

"The pump makes the machine breathe for him pulling his diaphragm out and then pushing it in again," she whispered. "Davie's completely paralyzed and can only speak when the machine exhales for him. Even then, he's talking less and less and I'm having a terrible time getting food into him because he chokes if he doesn't swallow to the rhythm of the machine."

Before following her to the kitchen he nodded at George whose smile twitched.

Alice busied herself putting the kettle on. "When he complained of an itch, I scratched it, and I caught his tears before they trickled into his ears." She turned to him, crossed her arms tightly across her chest and looked up at him with moist eyes. "Now he doesn't complain, he barely reacts."

She looked up at the ceiling and shook her head sighing, "Mike's not a bad man, Bear." She fell back against the kitchen counter, "We'd been married for ten years and given up hope of having children when I became pregnant. I don't know how other people react to having children but for Mike and me, David is the universe, the continuation, the reason we exist. And then polio struck and for a whole year we have had to lie in bed listening to that pump push and pull, push and pull, never stopping, trying, trying to make David's little lungs work for themselves." Her voice choked to a halt, and she chewed back tears. "Helplessness is a desperate matter. You are forever trying to grasp that invisible thing that is sure to solve or at the very least alleviate suffering, but is just out of range. It made Mike angry, and the anger drove him to drink. Do you think a judge would understand the circumstances?" She busied herself making coffee, put it down on the kitchen table and gestured him to sit in one of the stiff kitchen chairs. "Being equally upset, I was little help to him."

He sipped his coffee. "Perhaps he might get a lighter sentence but you have to understand, Alice, that Mike will be in prison for a good long time." The harsh truth even presented with sympathy made her squeeze her eyes tight over the escaping tears. "I've spoken to The Captain and he promises that Legion will donate the money from the Spring Square Dance to help you with finances. The question is can you hold on until then?"

She looked away from him. "I'm fine for the moment, Bear. I received money from an anonymous donor."

Of course, she had. He bet one of the donors couldn't even spell 'anonymous'.

They sipped their coffee in silence, she, not wanting to look him directly in the eye. With each tilt of her cup, he watched a change come over her: her eyes slit with determination and her back stiffened. "I'll just have to manage without him. Thank goodness for good friends," She hesitated. "Like you and Malcolm."

And a pair of 'anonymous' rogues.

She took him to the door, rested her cheek on the jamb and gave him a wry smile. "I couldn't have made it through the month without help, Bear. You do understand, don't you?"

Oh, yes! He understood all right. He tilted his head and stared up at her smile. "You're an islander aren't you, Alice?"

"I am," she said. "How did you know?"

"Just a guess." He wasn't going to mention her white, white teeth. "Then you've known George and Speaker for a long time."

"All my life."

Of course.

He drove to the sandy beach, which would be empty in the still cool weather. Leaving heavy footprints with every step he ploughed along sometimes taking a vicious kick at a stone. Now, what should he do? The Boys' theft hurt no one. Sure, Joe McTavish couldn't talk on his damned phone for a day, but was the crime worth a severe punishment? Wasn't it more important to help keep the Mason child alive? He did not want to arrest The Boys. If he did, Joe McTavish, a master of indignation, would demand justice. Will The Boys take a step too far one of these days? The hell with it.

By using the forward and noisy reverse gears, George nursed his big boat close enough for Speaker to leap out and, attach the stern rope. With the second rope, he moved towards the bow pretending he was unaware of Bear's presence.

"Morning, Boys. I wonder if I might have a word with you." Speaker looked at Bear with an expression of feigned curiosity, but a smile appeared on George's whole face; crinkled eyes and white teeth around an incorrigible smile.

George climbed out of the boat. "Something wrong Bear?"

The innocent looks that appeared on their faces were laughable.

"On Tuesday The Island Boat was here all night. Hope you two weren't getting into trouble." Bear helped Speaker attach the bow rope.

"Us?" Speaker sounded shocked at the suggestion.

"Important business." George whispered "Why do you ask, Bear? Has something happened?"

"There's always something, Boys."

"We weren't involved in anything!" Speaker insisted." We were on private business."

"What was this private business? If I might ask."

"I'm sorry, Bear, but it was private."

"Are there any witnesses who can say where you were?"

With his hat in his hand George wiped his brow while smiling, "Lots of witnesses. We were in Orville."

"At the whorehouse?"

"Not much else in Orville," Speaker tilted his head to the side and grinned. "So we're in the clear for whatever happened?" Speaker asked.

"I'll have to check at the whorehouse."

He turned away from them and over his shoulder said, "Why don't you two come up to my boathouse for a beer?" Out of the corner of his eye he saw The Boys look at each other with frowns, shrug and begin to follow him.

Speaker perched on the edge of the chair on his deck, and leaned forward on the arms, with an air of innocence. George looked more relaxed. They each accepted the proffered beers.

"Good view," Speaker said. "Guess you can see everything that goes on in the harbour,"

Bear took a sip of his beer. "Did you hear that someone stole all the copper telephone wires on the 5th concession?"

George's eyes widened with obviously feigned surprise but he couldn't hold back the twitch on his upper lip. "Did you catch the guy?"

"Nope, I didn't, and Bob McTavish has called in the Provincials. Those guys will chew on the problem till it's solved." Bear sat down in the third chair, tilted it back, and took another swig of his beer. "Whoever did it had best cover their steps well or they'll find themselves under arrest."

Speaker was the first to find his voice. "But you're our local cop! Why hand the investigation over to the provincial police?"

"I may be forced to. And I'm quite sure I know who the culprits are." Bear was enjoying himself at their expense.

"Best you explain." George croaked.

"I visited Alice Mason, you two know that, because George saw me there, and found that she was being helped by an 'anonymous' donor. I'll not give you the names of the men I suspect but think it would be too bad if they were arrested for doing their version of a good deed.

"It was a good deed, wasn't it? The kid is in an iron lung and Mason is off to Kingston Penitentiary for who knows how long." George whispered.

"For a good long time. The thing is, even if I don't agree, in 1950

Robin Hood generosity doesn't work. You can't commit a crime even if it's for a good cause, and expect to get away with it."

"Some do, sometimes," George looked out over the water. "And running that iron lung is expensive as hell!"

"That it is. And copper brings a good price these days, doesn't it?"

"Wouldn't know," George smiled and sipped his beer

"Seems to me," Speaker insisted, "A day or two without telephone ain't too serious. Hell, we have no phones on the island."

"And we like it that way." George croaked. "Gossip's a disease. Telephones spread it."

Bear laughed. "And you two would definitely not appreciate interference into your private businesses."

"Damned right!"

"I hope those criminals are smart enough to hide their tracks."

They finished their beers and got up to go. "Thanks for the beer. It was good talking to you." Speaker shook his hand, as did Whispering George.

Bear pushed his fingers through his mop of hair. He watched their backs as they descend the stairs. He would probably come to regret this but what else should he do?

The lake slowly swallowed the sun. Bear sipped his beer and watched the rippling path of light accompany its decent. There were many wonderful things about living in his boathouse but to sit on the porch over the harbour and the lake and watch God every evening was incomparable. He sat on his deck unmoving. When the final glow slipped beyond the horizon he was left at peace; at one with the world. And then he blinked.

He thought about the boys, their pursuit of freedom from life's restrictions, and smiled to himself. Crimes like theirs had a touch of art. He went inside, shut the glass door to the outside, and, in his small kitchen fished food out of his fridge and began to prepare his dinner, chopping onions and mushrooms to fry up and throw over his steak. The only passion he could police was his own, and he damn well would. In his own way.

No matter how early he arrived at work, Clara Seaborne preceded him. He touched her shoulder as he entered his office. She handed him the latest edition of The Cedartown Express. "Jumper's at it again."

THIEVES STEAL COPPER TELEPHONE WIRES.

Thieves cut down and stole all the wires on the 5th concession leaving everyone in the area without telephone service for more than 24 hours.

Bob McTavish, whose acreage is on the 5th has demanded the assistance of the provincial police saying they have 'more expertise' in dealing with this kind of situation. An insult, one would think to our own Bear McKinley who is responsible for the area.

Bell Telephone has replaced all the wires and phones are once more, functioning.

So, what if the little jockey goes after him? There's truth in what he and Bob McTavish had to say. He's acting more like a social worker than a cop. If the provincials are unhappy with him so be it. The decision about his future will be made for him, before he's forced to arrest the likes of George and Speaker.

"But turn to page two, "Clara called from the outer office, laughing as she said it.

When he did, he, too, burst out laughing. There was a photo of The Chief, in the middle of the river dressed in waders holding a pickerel on the end of his spear. The caption was titled: The DEFENDER OF OUR LAWS

The poor Chief," Bear called out to Clara.

She came to the door. "It's fortunate that around here the folks have a good sense of humour. The Chief will suffer a hell of a lot of teasing, but nothing will happen to him or his position. Most of us will just appreciate a good laugh."

"Not like Toronto." Bear mumbled.

"Laughter's harder to find amongst all those tall buildings."

Chapter 10

Driving along the lakeshore road, Bear saw the truck of Frenchie. He stopped his cruiser beside the rotund man who was dressed in waders topped with dirty navy pants and shirt.

"Big job, Frenchie?"

The French man removed a shovel from the back of the truck. "The customer, he has not cleaned his tank in years. I'll be up to my arse in shit." He started towards the house with a backward wave to Bear.

Bear shook his head. No wonder the guy went on drunken sprees.

Since he was down on the lakeshore road he thought he might as well drop in to see Malcolm. Or maybe he shouldn't, as Tess was sure to be there. He definitely shouldn't.

There was nobody on the back porch but he heard Essie wailing from within. He opened the screen door, leaned into the kitchen and saw Tess standing at the counter eating a piece of toast laden with butter and jam. "Bear!"

"That's a mighty noise for a small child. Is everything alright?"

"I don't know what's up. Mother is closeted with Essie in the bedroom and won't let anyone in. It's probably just some small drama. Essie is good at that." She put her toast down and came to the door.

"Do you think there's anything I could do?"

She pushed him back out onto the screened porch. "Not here, but you could take me for a ride in your cruiser." Her head was tilted and her smile innocently flirtatious.

She had jam at the corner of her mouth. He wiped it away with his finger. He shouldn't have done that. She kept her head tilted towards him waiting for a second touch. He retreated to the screen door. "I came to say hello to your father. Where is he?"

There was a tease in her pout and the way she looked up at him from a lowered brow. "No ride in your cruiser?"

"No ride."

"Daddy is in one of his black moods. He went off in the car."

"I'll talk to him later." Bear escaped quickly. It was not until he got into the cruiser that he realized the wailing within the house had been reduced to breath-catching sobs. Little ones find every drama world shattering, and, in effect, he supposed, it was for them, each experience being a new piece of knowledge, that adds to their sad exposure to life. Obviously, the latest addition was not a positive one.

At the end of the lakeshore road there was a curve towards the lake and along the water's edge ending at the harbour. Bear saw Malcolm's car parked on the road; pulled up behind it and climbed down the bank to the sandy beach looking for his friend. He found him sitting on a rock, smoking and staring out at the lake. He didn't move when Bear approached nor did his eyes appear to blink.

Bear crouched down, swept the beach for pebbles, methodically flipped some into the water, but said nothing.

Suddenly aware of Bear, Malcolm ground his butt into the sand and took another sweet caporal from the package and lit it with shaking hands "Didn't see you there, Bear." He stared out at the water. "Too busy fighting the lion!

"The lion?"

"Yes, god damned it, and it's getting closer each day."

Bear watched as his friend made a supreme effort to push the monster back down, deep down behind thought.

Malcolm stood, yanked at the back of his pants, laughed an artificial laugh, and pulled on his ear.

Together they stared out at the ripples and Bear waited in silence to give Malcolm time "Come for a drive, the wind might blow some fresh air through your thoughts." They got in the cruiser. "George and Speaker are causing a lot of activity over at the other side of the harbour. They're probably up to something. Let's go and check."

Even before they arrived, Bear and Malcolm could see an unusual amount of scurrying down by the Wawanesa, "What in Hell are those two up to now?" He was laughing a real laugh even before they got out of the car.

Speaker was there trying to catch a piglet that had escaped from his arms; it's little feet wind-milling it along in a zigzag pattern that was a test for an alcohol-addled, two- hundred-pound man. In a flying leap, which landed him on his stomach, he caught the tail of the squeaking animal, and pulled. it into his chest. Up on his knees he showed the piglet to Bear. "Behold the future of our riches, Bear."

"What are you up to now?"

"George and I are going into the pork business!"

"I'll be goddamned," The Captain laughed.

With his hands on his hips and a shake of the head Bear asked, "You mean raise pigs?"

"That's right."

"I'm surprised you have the money for it."

"We don't. Ask George, he'll explain it better than me." Bear and Malcolm went over to George who was straddling a box holding two more piglets while collecting down payments from 'investors', a group of perhaps twenty men who were gathered around him. "What'll you feed them?" One asked.

"Corn, grass, roots, and we'll get fruit and vegetable garbage from The Brown Jug." He croaked. "We'll fatten them up well."

"Are they vaccinated?"

"Of course, they're vaccinated. Wouldn't buy these little babies any other way."

"And wormed?"

George scratched his chin. "We'll have it done."

"And where will you keep them?" Another questioned.

"In my barn at the back of the island." He held up the flat of his hand, "But when you come to visit your pig we'll bring it to the harbour so you don't have to dirty yourself galumphing through the woods." With his unshaved face, and flannel shirt in which the plaid was faded, George, somehow, still appeared an impressive entrepreneur and the audience listened. Must be his sinewy body impressive English, and sincere expression that made him sound like a business executive. The deceptive devil!!!

Bear waited until the "investors' had paid their money and had left in satisfaction. "Explain this undertaking to me, George." He scratched his head. "Seems to me you've said you're always broke. Where did you get the money for this venture?

"'Course we're broke. That's why we're selling these piglets as an investment. We'll feed them and fatten them, then when they're slaughtered the owners will get their meat fresh."

"You'll have them butchered, too?"

"We're working on that."

"I'm impressed, He looked down at the box. How many have you got there?".

"We'll start with three. Each one of these little devils is a different breed. That way our investors have a choice. This one," he said, taking Speaker's captured all white pig into his arms and tickling its erect ears "Is a Yorkshire. And here in the box is a Duroc that's all red and a Hampshire that's black and white."

"Have you sold any piglets?"

"'Course we have! When they learn that these babies can grow to 250 pounds and they understand that we can sell the beasts for 30 cents a pound they realize that their investment will pay off!"

"How much are you charging them?"

"Only a hundred dollars a piglet. Think of the profit they're in for!"

"And where do you and Speaker profit?"

"On the sale of the piglets, and, of course we've got to charge for the feed and the care of the little critters. And if they want to visit them they'll have to buy a ticket on the Island boat. So far we've sold 25 and that's just the beginning!"

"How much did you pay for them?"

"Not much. That's why it's such a good deal." He waved the wad of cash. "We'll send some of this to Alice for the boy."

Bear wandered over to the box and peered in.

George put Speaker's piglet in the box and took a pad from his pocket to record the names and amounts of those who had given him a down payment. More cars were arriving with potential 'investors' or as Bear suspected, 'victims' and Speaker was calling as they got out of their cars, "If you want one you'd best put your name in now, they're going fast!"

Bear shook his head and turned towards his cruiser.

Chapter 11

Summer

"Did you take our Pig Earnings to Alice?" Speaker asked as he loaded garbage into the Wawanesa."

"I did, and it's agony seeing that little tyke struggle for air. I kept inhaling deeper myself. His desperation is contagious."

"Yep, it hurts like Hell to watch him," Speaker answered as he continued loading. He looked up at the sound of a truck. "Looks like Marvin McTavish wants to visit his pig."

George pulled out his tattered book. "Let's see here. He bought a Yorkshire. That's Bessie, the white one.

"That's good." Speaker answered as he watched McTavish climb down from his truck and start towards the boat. "Bessie followed us to the harbour this morning. She's probably still wandering around in the area. We'll grab her and Marvin can view her right there at the dock."

"There's someone with him

"It's Skip McNeil. I hope to hell he didn't buy a Yorkshire, too." George checked his notes. "Nope, we're o.k. He bought the Duroc. That's Trudi, but I don't know where the hell she's wandered off to. Speaker, you go looking for her and I'll entertain them till you get back with the sows."

"Coming to visit your investment Boys?" Speaker helped them on to the boat.

"Damned right we are." Skip replied. "Want to make sure you're fattening them up, good." They climbed into the Island Boat.

"That'll be a dollar for the crossing," George whispered, and extended his hand.

"You two have a good thing going," Marvin complained as he removed a dollar from his wallet. "What's the rotten smell?"

"That's garbage from the Brown Jug. Elsa gives it to us to fatten up the pigs."

"It sure does stink."

"That stink, means money in your pocket, Mister."

On their arrival at the island harbour George invited them to share some hooch while Speaker went to fetch their pigs for viewing.

"Don't worry about that," Skip replied, "We can go to your barn," and set out to follow Speaker.

George grabbed him by the arm. "It's a tricky path and there are some mighty snakes in the woods." He pulled Skip back and put his arm around the shoulders of each man. "Best you come and have a nip and let Speaker do the job."

In the upended Wawanesa The First, which they had turned into a makeshift office at the head of the harbour, George took a couple of smudged glasses, wiped them out with his shirttail and poured the men a good glug of his homemade brew.

Skip took a gulp, grimaced, shivered and cried. "God damned it, this will knock my socks off!"

Marvin chose to go slower.

Speaker caught Bessie and Trudi in the first five minutes, but was wise enough to wait until George's entertainment had its effect. He lay down on the ground and let the pigs scrounge in the grass around him. The trees above him were shimmering in the wind, puffy clouds sailed through the sky and the moss under his head formed a perfect pillow.

He had no idea how long he'd slept. "It's time to go girls." He leashed the pair and they sauntered down the path to the harbour. At about 100 pounds each, his girls were not exactly speedy.

At the 'office', the investors, six sheets to the wind, were swaying on the stoop, awaiting the arrival of their investments.

"Here they are gentlemen." Speaker presented the pigs. "As you can see your shares are increasing by the day. At 30 cents, a pound, they are already worth more than what you paid and they've a lot of growing to go still!"

"Well damned me!" Marvin slurred. "That's the prettiest pig I've ever seen. Look at that pink snout, and her long lashes. She could win a beauty contest."

"Nah!" Skip argued. "My golden girl has it all over your white virgin." He pushed at Marvin's shoulder.

The two began to scuffle.

"Gentlemen! Now that you've seen your sows, I should take them back to the barn."

Marvin fell on his knees and embraced Bessie. "Don't pay any attention to the SOB," he looked up at Speaker. "Does she have a name?"

"Bessie."

"Bessie, you are the most beautiful pig in the whole world."

Skip swayed above his animal, too drunk to lean over

Speaker looked up at George standing in the doorway. George scraped his hand across his stubble. "Those pigs must have been on the other side of the island."

"Opposite ends," Speaker prevaricated.

"I wanna take my girl home." Skip grabbed the pig's tail and starts to pull.

Speaker released Skip's hand from the complaining sow. "I should get these girls back to the barn. George will take you home."

George steered the bleary-eyed pair to his boat. "It'll cost you anther dollar for the return trip."

"Why can't I take my pig?"

That evening they sat in in the open back of the Wawanesa, laughing as they reviewed the day's activities. George pleasured in the delight of their unrestrained laughter. When they caught their breath, he croaked. "But summer weather will bring more investors wanting to see their babies." Unable to release his smile he added, "Something will have to be done, cousin."

Speaker thought on it. "Maybe the Island Boat should break down. We can go back and forth with the motor boat."

"So can they." George said. "We'll have to think of some big god damned disaster that kills them all, and we'd better do it fast. Could be we've stepped over Bear's line this time."

"But the money's for Alice, he'll get that."

"Not sure." Hands on knees, George looked down, mentally playing with thoughts of Bear and what he might do. "So far he has bent for us, but this may be too much."

Speaker reached behind him for the hooch, took a gulp and handed it to George. They sat silent.

After contemplating the problem George turned to Speaker and with a half-smile said, "I think diarrhea is pretty nasty in pigs."

"How do we find out?"

"That's what libraries are for isn't it?"

"We can't go to the Cedartown Library and ask for a book about pig diseases."

"Sure we can. We have pigs and we worry." George sipped his beer. "I'll go tomorrow."

The next day, Library books in hand they pushed aside dirty dishes and George read. "Says here pigs are susceptible to intestinal diseases and diarrhea is the most common sign."

"We could say they all died of it." Speaker suggested.

"Says here, porcine circovirus type 2 causes high fevers, breathing difficulties, coughing and sneezing and they go off their feed."

George pushed back his chair and started pacing. "That's it! The poor pigs caught the disease one by one and it broke our hearts but we had to kill the whole drift to save the only surviving pigs, Bessie, Sport and Trudi?"

"Drift?"

George took opened the book. "Says here a bunch of young pigs is called a drift."

"And we burned the bones to make sure the infection didn't dawdle in the bones of the three who survived!"

"Right! And we threw the ashes in the lake."

They shook hands, proud of their brilliance and sat in silence mulling over possible complications.

For days, they rehashed their story and then announced their sad tale at the Little Brown Jug.

"I'm so sorry, Boys," Elsa sympathized, "I was impressed with your business acumen."

George and Speaker looked downcast, as though they were on the verge of tears.

"You lost the whole herd?" Bear asked."

"It's a drift, not a herd," Speaker corrected him.

"We were able to save three but the rest just withered away. George answered. "We burned the corpses to make sure the dead bodies didn't leave any disease behind."

"It was so sad we had a bit of a funeral for them. Said some 'ashes to ashes' words before we dumped them in the lake" Speaker added.

"What are you going to tell your investors?"

"We've been thinking a lot on that," Speaker said.

"Were you insured?"

"'Course not." George croaked. "But our investors have to understand that they took a gamble, and unfortunately it failed."

"It certainly did! Bear stared at the pair and they returned his stare with wide-eyed innocence.

George's smile remained sad and without a twitch.

"Nevertheless, when Bessie and Dinah and Sport are full grown and sold we'll get a little money to pay them back some of their investment." George answered. "You see Bear, they won't be out of pocket a whole lot."

"And you two will have made money on the original sales and the tickets to and from the island for those who wanted to visit their pigs as they fattened."

George leaned on the restaurant bar looking very serious. "That's the thing, Bear." Then his smile did twitch. "There is always a gamble when you're trying to multiply your winnings by a big percentage."

Bear waved away their explanations.

Chapter 12

Three miles north of Cedartown the lake shore road was bounded by railway tracks running along the edge of the lake on the left and fields on the right. There were white caps on the lake, and the wheat in the fields was bending in the wind. It was the end of a slow day and Clara had invited Bear to the farm for dinner.

Stone pillars at the entrance stood precariously having lost a lot of mortar, He turned into the lane, which led directly to the barn at the end, but before reaching the faded red buildings, he turned on to a secondary lane that wound around to a large, very old brick house that had been in Clara's husband, Andrew's family since it was built in the 1800's. A huge peeling white-painted veranda swept around the front and sides giving it a solid, if aging, elegance.

Careful to avoid the ancient hitching post that had the carved head of a horse, and the huge wrought iron pots full of flaming flowers and greens, Bear parked and stepped out of the car. On the porch, he jumped back at the possibility of attack by flapping birds as they escaped from drooping nests perched between the antlers of the moose and deer heads that were hung on the brick wall.

Michael, Clara and Andrew's adopted son appeared around the corner of the porch and slid to a stop when he saw Bear. "Officer McKinley!" He blushed.

"Michael.'

The boy looked down and toed the planks of wood.

Bear had caught Michael and his friends playing an inebriated game of chicken, challenging each other from opposite ends of Lakeshore Rd. Two cars had ended up in the ditch. But, fortunately, no one was hurt.

"Saturday nights with your gang are going to get you in deep trouble if you keep up with nonsense like last week's escapade."

"I know, I know, sometimes I just need to have my heart race a little." He picked a leaf off the bush at the edge of the porch and tossed it. "I love Clara and Andrew, but there are times I need to escape the ploughing and haying, and milking and egg-collecting: the same monotonous tune, over and over."

"You've just graduated from high school? Are you going to college?"

"I guess so. I've been accepted at Guelph, but I really don't want to study agriculture."

"I'm sure there are other courses."

"There are but I don't want to hurt Andrew who has done so much for me."

Bear put his arm over the strapping boy's shoulder, feeling the strength of the young man. And handsome he was too, with a lock of hair falling over his forehead and blue eyes shaded with black lashes. "You'll figure it out. The college will open-up options you haven't even thought of. Now let's go and be fed."

They started down the long, wide hall that led to the kitchen. The walls were covered in dark wall paper that was peeling a little in the corners and old intricately carved furniture lined both walls.

The huge kitchen at the end of the hall had all the warmth that the front lacked. Andrew a big chested, rosy- cheeked man sat at the table smoking his pipe. He stood up and shook Bear's hand. "Welcome, Officer McKInley. I'm ashamed we haven't had you here before."

"Thanks for having me, Andrew." He looked over at Clara cooking at the stove, "And Clara." He sniffed the odours. "Smell's delicious!

"Nice to have you, Bear. It will be ready in a minute."

Bear looked around the kitchen. It had a huge wood stove in the middle, an obvious addition to the old place as the large fireplace and wall oven beside it looked unused. The sink was wood, and it still had a hand pump on the side although there were now taps as well. The sun shining through the window on one side brightened the soft comfort of cushioned chairs, light wood cupboards and linoleum floor. "This is quite a house, Andrew. When was it built?"

"1815. Built by my ancestor and has remained in the family ever since. It has quite a history." Andrew went on to talk of the poor Scotsman and the daughter of pensioned off Englishman who fell in love, built the place and had a fox and Percheron horse farm. "You can still see the foundations of the fox farm in the woods. They were dug deep to prevent the animals from escaping."

"I don't even know the names of my great-grandparents. This place, it's roots, your ancestors, all of it, must be comforting."

"It's home," Andrew smiled a wan smile. "And it makes demands that are sometimes hard to keep."

Bear sensed from the solidity of the man, that Andrew's aside was all he would hear about the difficulties they were having. There had to be huge demands made of a place like this, a home in which memories of generations are imbedded into the walls. Did the responsibility outweigh their love of the place or was the reverse true? He knew Clara's salary was necessary to keep the farm running.

The meal continued comfortably

"Why did you want to be a policeman?" Michael asked with curiosity."

What could he say? In the heat of youth, he imagined he would be a protector of the public and even save some lives. But dust has settled on his ideals. He pushed himself up from his chair, "To keep the world safe from hellions like you," he teased. "I'm sorry to have to leave, Clara and Andrew. I've enjoyed every minute of it."

Clara saw him out.

"You have a great family, Clara."

"Thanks Bear. I stupidly thought that as Michael grew older our worries would diminish but I was wrong."

"You know, there's an opening at the pier for an assistant swimming instructor. Maybe it would be good for Michael to get away from the farm for a while. Young Tess Fraser is working there now and seems to enjoy it." Perhaps she would be drawn to Michael and leave him alone.

"I'll mention it to him."

Bear got in the car and wound down the window. Clara, leaned in on her elbows."

"You've been around a long time, Clara. Do you remember a girl named Cassandra Warren?"

"Haven't heard of her in years. I remember her more by reputation. It was said that as a teenager she was rather loose with her affections, but I can't be sure her reputation wasn't exaggerated by the hollow boasting of young men." She looked over his shoulder and inward. "I do remember that she and George were inseparable and a very handsome pair they were too, he with his height and beautiful body and she with wild hair, a huge smile and oozing sex appeal. They were island kids, and looked down on by the locals, considered to be a bit backward and incestuous. Why do you ask?"

"This is for your ears only and I'm telling you because you will need to know. Bear squeezed his lips together wondering how to say it all and keep Cass in a good light. "Cass is now the Madam of the most expensive brothel in Toronto."

Clara stared unblinking then smiled an uncertain smile, and shook her head. "I'm speechless!"

"I'm telling you this for a reason, Clara." Bear spoke without humour. "Cass bought the old White Farm on the island as a place to where she can escape, if she is exposed, because there is a criminal element that would be very worried she might reveal a lot of the things she knows. She could be in danger."

"Cassandra Warren! I find it hard to absorb!"

"She's a good woman Clara, at least in my book. It just happened that she was very good at selling sex." He wiped his hand around the steering wheel. "Without her help I'd be off the police force entirely." He related his own tale, and then continued in a serious tone. "I'm only making you aware of a possible future danger. She has no intention of giving up the business unless forced to."

"I'm sure George knows all about this."

"Of course he does. The first time we met he said of Cass, 'I love her and it's no fun."

"It's hard to take all this in. If the worst happens, what is it you want of me, Bear?"

"I'm sure I'll need a lot of help. Most important would be to keep the secret of her whereabouts from being leaked."

"As long as they were made aware of danger to Cass, I'm sure the townspeople would make a point of keeping the information of her whereabouts from outsiders."

"Let's wait and see and hope none of this happens."

Two days later Clara peeked her head into Bear's office and announced, "The Provincial Police Chief phoned to say he's on his way over."

Bear was not sure whether to offer his superior his chair behind the desk or one in front so he remained standing until the Chief selected the visitor's chair. He fingered the Cedartown Express lying on Bear's desk.

"That little twit is out to get you," McKinley.

"Looks like it, Sir." Bear couldn't hold back a grin, "I guess I'm not the only one."

The Chief threatened him with his finger. "Don't you say a damn word!"

"No Sir. I wouldn't dare Sir." He bit his teeth over his lower lip to restrain the escaping smile.

The Chief smiled and shook his head. "This one I'll never be able to live down."

"As I see it, Sir, it's good for the town to be able to have a laugh at authority and they'll love you all the more for being human."

The Chief harrumphed and shook his head. "Hope to hell you're right." He sat down and pulled out his briefcase, and looked over the reports that Bear had submitted. "What's the latest on the copper wire theft?"

"I've been to Newmarket to see who is buying the copper but of course they are mum: why reveal an excellent source?"

"Joe McTavish has been on our back, wanting us to solve the problem."

"I don't know, Sir. Joe McTavish is full of such resentment and indignation he would have the perpetrators sent to prison for life. I find it's a petty crime that doesn't deserve a lot of attention." He looked into the Chief's eyes. "That's not to say, I won't pursue the problem. It's just not high up on my list."

The Chief nodded. "You're a good man, Bear. I'd like to put you up for a transfer, and probably a promotion." He pointed at the newspaper article, "Having had my own problems with that camera-carrying piece of shit I am not the least bit interested in what he prints." The Chief sat forward, elbows on the chair and hands clasped in front of him. "I really came to feel you out. I'll transfer you as soon as possible, but only if you're serious about continuing in law enforcement." He pointed to the newspaper. "Those articles paint a picture of a man who is a little unsure of himself."

Leave Cedartown? Leave Elsa, Malcolm, The Boys and the characters? It would relieve him of Tess. Did he want that? "You're right, Chief, I find it tough being a cop when exposed to the desperation of men like Mike Mason."

"You wouldn't have let Mike Mason go?"

"Of course not. But I hope a good lawyer will elicit some sort of sympathy by explaining the cause of his drunkenness."

"That's not our job."

"Of course it's not. But, I fear, neither is it the job of Mistress Law."

"Sounds like the job of a cop is weighing on you." The Chief stood up and wandered over to Bear's window that looked out on to Main Street. "I think every good cop in the country has suffered your present moment and had to deal with the uncertainty that pervades our profession." He turned and looked down at Bear who had remained seated and was staring up at his boss. "It's a tough decision, and I'll understand whatever you decide."

"Don't know what I want to do, but for the moment, I'd prefer to stay in Cedartown." There, he did it. "I'm grateful, but could you hold on to your offer for a while?"

"Of course I could." He stood up and tapped the newspaper. "If you can stand the notoriety of that piece of shit, I won't interfere."

"I'm relying on the citizens to think the same of him as you do."

"Good luck then."

What had he done? Was he watering the tendrils of roots? Is that what he wanted??

Chapter 13

Bear was waiting when George pulled in with the Wawanesa. The policeman was biting his lower lip and staring into space. George stiffened. Before even waiting for Speaker to tie the boat he mouthed the question, "Cass?"

Bear nodded, held up the Toronto Star and turned towards his boathouse.

"Can you finish up here, Speaker. I want to speak to Bear about something." Without waiting for a reply, he followed Bear's back.

In the boathouse, Bear handed him the paper.

Toronto Brothel Exposed and Closed

Forest Hill residents expressed shock and surprise that for years, a brothel had been in business in one of the mansions on Randall Rd., Reporters lined the street watching the prostitutes being escorted out in handcuffs.

The Madam, Cass Warren, who was the owner of the house responded to questions as she was being led away.

"Who were your clients, Cass?"

"All your best friends, My Dear." Her smile suggested she was without a care in the world.

The woman's statement told the whole story. She and her girls were released without charges, and when she left the building was asked. "Who are your special friends Madam?" Standing tall, she just shook her head and smiled.

"You must have hated what you did? Were you forced into it?"

"I enjoyed every bit of it." She got into a taxi and opened the window. "Hell, I might even write a book about it and call it 'The Carefree Call Girl'!".

She began to roll up the window. "A good title, don't you think?" She frowned and tilted her head. "Maybe 'The Merry Madam' would be better." She laughed and waved and turned away from them.

The article included a photo of Cass talking to the reporter as her girls were climbing into taxis to get away from the scene.

George let the newspaper drop to his knees. "She should never have mentioned a book." He got up. "We have to use your office phone to call her. It's the only one that's not on a party line."

"And where will we phone? Do you think she'll be allowed back in the house?"

"Let's try and then I'll go to the city and fetch her."

Bear was quiet for a moment. "I'll go with you. Cass could be in danger."

Clara Seaborne jumped from her chair so fast it almost tilted over. "You have a visitor, Bear."

Her smile was indecipherable "Your friend."

George made a dash for Bear's office, and by the time Bear had entered George had Cass in a giant hug. "You are a fool My Cass," he croaked. "You should never has said that you might write a book."

Cass pulled away and shook Bear's hand with both of hers. "You're right Georgie, I should have kept my mouth shut," she tilted her head and gave a naughty smile, "Even if it is true."

"We have to get her to the island fast, Bear." George nervously pulled at Cass's hand.

"Slow down, Georgie. We have time," she soothed. "There's nobody out there trying to get me, at least not yet."

"How can you be sure?" George felt prickles all over his skin. This was worse than war. "Please, let's go Cass. I can't let anything happen to you." He looked at Bear. "In your cruiser, it's safer."

"Wait! I brought a truck full of things with me. We'll have to get them in the Wawanesa. It will take time."

"Where's your truck? I'll take it down to the harbour and meet you there." He practically pushed the pair towards the door.

"Wait!" Bear grabbed his arm, and pulled him back. He looked over George's tense shoulder. "Clara, come here please!"

When his secretary squeezed past George he asked her, "Have they read the Star article at the Little Brown Jug?"

"Not only there, all over town," she answered.

"Think about it, George. If anyone sees Cass, Jumper will find out and she'll never have peace!"

George returned to the office, collapsed in a chair, and cried, "What can we do?" His voice cracked like pine cones in a fire.

"If you're agreeable, Cass. I'll get you to my boathouse where we can wait until the middle of the night to take you over."

"It's not Cedartown I'm worried about, except for that twit Jumper. It's the dangerous people who might find out where she is."

Cass put her arm around George's shoulder. "Georgie's right, let's at least try to preserve my privacy."

Bear nodded in agreement. "Then I suggest that you do the regular run with the Wawanesa, George, and then come back after dark."

"Speaker can do the run. I'll go with you. You take Cass in the cruiser and I'll bring her truck down to the harbour, but I'm sure as hell not leaving Cass for any longer than that."

In the cruiser Cass, with a hat pulled down over her forehead looked around at Cedartown. "It's interesting to be back"

"I understood from George that you preferred to avoid Cedartown and that's why you had builders from the other side of the lake.

"It's not that I don't like Cedartown, quite the opposite actually, I love its solidity; the way the stores are dug in to the earth with no special attractions. They seem to say, 'we are what we are, take us or leave us'. It just doesn't suit my need for excitement." She leaned back on the seat. "But, while I'm here, I am going to write my memoir, and I need privacy to do so. After that I probably will disappear for a while. The news will make a lot of people nervous."

"Is that why you're writing it?"

"I'm writing it for various reasons, Bear. First and foremost, for the money it will bring in: money I'll need since the authorities have closed down my business: second, because this tight-assed society needs to learn about the enjoyment of sex in all its forms, and finally, because I love shocking society."

"It will be a best seller, I'm sure."

"When it's done I think I'll go to Europe for a while."

"But you've bought property here."

"And I will use it, but the peace of the place will infect me from time to time and I'll have to go off and rattle the world a bit." She looked out the window. "George is really worried that, at worst, I'm playing with danger and at the very least paparazzi or over-sexed idiots will try and get to the island."

"You shouldn't have any problems out there. It's pretty isolated." He looked over at her, astounded at how relaxed she appeared. "If you ever need supplies I'd suggest you send a note to Clara Seaborn to make all the purchases. George and Speaker might decipher your needs in an incomprehensible fashion!"

She laughed. "And I can count on Mrs. Seaborn to be quiet about the whole thing?"

"Clara Seaborn has more secrets tucked away in that mighty head than anyone else in Cedartown. You can rely on her."

George and Cass sat on the edge of the harbour with their feet dangling close to the water. Clara and Bear stood above them.

"I feel as though I'm in a novel. Here we are at 4.00 a.m. at the Cedartown Harbour," Clara smiled down at Cass, "with a now famous madam who is to be escorted to a secret lair by two suspect rogues." Clara shook her head and laughed. "It's really quite unbelievable."

"Could be anyone who gets involved with Cass is stepping away from everyday life."

"And I'm grateful to every one of you." Cass replied.

They lapsed into silence as they awaited the boat.

"It's so still," Clara whispered. "The water is like glass and there's not a chirp from a bird."

"Waiting for the moon to release its hold," George mumbled. "This time of the day doesn't belong to us." He stopped and listened. "I hear the Wawanesa."

It took a few minutes for the others to hear. "I'll bring the truck to the edge," George whispered.

Trying to make as little noise as possible, their whispered moves were loud in the surrounding silence. Once the boat was packed everyone but Clara jumped in. Cass reached out and took her hand. "Thanks for everything, Clara."

"Not a bit of it," Clara insisted, "I've enjoyed every minute of this clandestine undertaking. And if you need any special purchases, just let me know. I'll take care of them."

Chapter 14

Instead of heading for the harbour, Bear aimed the boat towards a shoal he knew and pulled out his fishing rod that was tucked along beside the oars. He'll just troll for a little while.

It had been a long night and morning. The Wawanesa couldn't dock at Cass's island home so Hawker, who was already there, had to travel back and forth with his motorboat collecting Cass and all her things.

He smiled remembering how Speaker had dandied himself up, obviously hoping Cass would appreciate him. There was a gentle nick in the man's intelligence that produced an appealing innocence. George, on the other hand was a set-apart man who was much more difficult to decipher. Both had extraordinarily white teeth: Cass too. He wondered whether there was something special in the island diet. Whatever it was, each one of them had charmingly deceptive smiles that easily seduced, and forgave their toying with the law. Bear smiled. He, like everyone, was a victim of their charm.

With the motor turned to its lowest speed he cast the line that had the river runt, his favorite lure on the end, and trolled on in long monotonous turns over the shoal, letting more and more line out as he went. He'd better be careful, as there were some rocks that could damage the engine. He had read the information Cass had sent and worried that if she even attempted to write about many of her suspicions there would be trouble. Hawker would keep an eye out for her but he and The Boys had best do some patrolling. Fishing would be a good excuse.

He felt a tug on the line and pulled back hard, but the fish escaped.

Reeling in, he recast and sat to steer the boat while gently tugging the line back and forth to attract a nice bass to his river runt.

In the distance, he could see the Cedartown pier. There was something about the town that wouldn't release him from its grasp, but God knew what it was. The place was certainly not beautiful. It did have an abundance of cedar both in hedges and trees and the grass was very green at this time of year, but the place was as flat as foolscap and there wasn't a house that was newer than twenty-five years of age, to say nothing of drab Main Street, which seemed determined to create an appearance that would not tempt tourists to stop. The town didn't give a damn about the outside world.

Still, he didn't feel imprisoned by the place. He could still move on, and probably would.

His rod bent with a bite and he jerked it to hook the fish then reeled it in slowly as it fought for release. He brought it into the boat and bonked the still flapping bass on the head before removing the hooks. It must be two pounds. It would make a good dinner. He'd better get back to work. After storing his rod, he drove carefully over the shoal before speeding up towards the harbour.

Entering the harbour he could see that swimming lessons were taking place on the other side of the pier. Tess had her class of little ones and didn't see his boat. Thank God!

Before entering his own boathouse, he drove over to the booth to refill the square red gas tank. Jack Winston, the owner, handed down the nozzle. "Been fishing?"

"Had business on the island but couldn't resist a troll at Jacobson's point.

"Catch anything?"

Bear held up the bass to show him and a camera flashed.

Jumper appeared from the other side of the pump.

"Still hiding behind your camera. Jumper? Why don't you put your weapon down for a while? Life is real on this side." He put the fish down, screwed the top on the tank, started the engine and without a word to Jumper, steered towards his own boathouse.

Having locked the door of his boathouse he headed towards his cruiser in the parking lot. Malcolm Fraser's car was parked looking out over the harbour and Bear went over to speak to him. He leaned down to look in the driver's window. Fraser was staring off into space and didn't acknowledge him. Bear knocked on the window but received no reaction. Strange, what was going on? He went around to the passenger side and got in. "Malcolm?" Still no reply: still staring off into space. Bear gently shook his shoulder. "Malcolm?"

He was staring into some unimaginable devastation. Tears rolled down his face.

Bear was not sure whether to stay or go. A man does not want an audience for his agonies, but he had to do something so he slipped in beside him and sat quietly. Perhaps just being here would bring him back; away from the horrors that won't leave him in peace. He stared out at the harbour. Here he sits trying to help a man in trouble and at the same he battles erotic thoughts about this man's beautiful child. He shakes his head in disgust with himself.

After a time, Bear, without taking his eyes from the brown water of the harbour interrupted Malcolm's frozen misery, "It seems the Boys have lost all their pigs to a deadly virus." The maneuverings of those two devils appealed to Malcolm.

Malcolm turned towards him and smiled a wry smile. "Knowing them, they never had the pigs in the first place."

It worked! "You're probably right.

"And you'll leave it alone?"

"Probably not. My curiosity won't let me."

"But you'll not go after The Boys?"

"No, but if I find proof, I'll hold it over them to keep them in line."

Malcolm's laugh was so hearty Bear felt he could leave. "I'd best go, Clara Seaborne is awaiting me."

Malcolm waved him off. Does he even remember his tears? Bear was not sure.

"Just a minute, Bear, Malcolm called from the car window. "What's that?" He pointed to the mouth of the Castor where it entered the harbour.

Following his finger Bear saw a green and brown pile which could be a dead branch, but there was something balloon-like in its appearance., Most of it lay unmoving but the ballooned section fought the flow of the river. "I hope it's not what I think it is." He jogged towards the union of harbour and river.

"It's a body. I'm sure it's a body!" Malcolm had followed him.

"Can't get at it from here. I'll get my boat. Will you call the provincials for me?"

"That's a shirt that's bubbling! He stared frozen. It's an army shirt –he's a soldier!" he stood there paralyzed.

Bear yelled him out of his reverie. "Malcolm, go to Jack Winston's booth and phone NOW!"

It was rocky and shallow where the river spilled into the harbour. By the time the provincials arrived Bear had managed to retrieve the body and deliver it to the waiting ambulance, where Jack Winston, Malcolm and other curious onlookers had gathered.

Unfortunately, Jumper was there to witness the tragedy and the click, clicking accompanied by camera flashes infuriated everyone and caused Malcolm to seethe. Between ground teeth he hissed, "You'd better damned well treat this with the dignity the poor man deserves, Mister!

Jumper didn't lift his face from behind the camera. "Looks like he either committed suicide, or was so drunk he fell. Can't think either death was very dignified."

Malcolm curled his fists and squeezed. "Where were you when he was fighting? How could you know what he suffered over there?" His nostrils flared in disgust before he turned away from the little man.

The dead man had a scraggly beard and a bad cut on his forehead. There was no identification in his pockets.

"Does anybody recognize him?" the captain asked as he watched the body being lifted into the ambulance.

"He's not from around here," Jack Winston rubbed his jaw, "I'd know if he was."

"That's an army shirt," Malcolm murmured. "Poor man, made it through and now this."

"We'll take it from here, Bear."

"You'll let me know what's up and if I can do anything on this end."

"Of course," the captain answered and waved as he climbed in his cruiser to follow the ambulance.

A week after finding the body, the captain phoned Bear.

"Looks like the man was a vagabond. We've not been unable to identify him and we found enough alcohol in his blood to make us think he fell higher up the river and floated down with the current."

"So that's it, then?"

"I'm afraid so. There's nothing more we can do unless we receive requests about a missing man."

"It's sad to let a life float off without recognition."

"It is that, but there's naught we can do, My Boy."

Thinking of Malcolm, he said "Makes you wonder if he was a soldier who was ruined by what he'd been through."

"It could easily be that. Nobody returns unchanged." The Captain answered with a husky voice. "But while I have you on the phone," he said in a lighter tone, "Have you thought about the promotion?"

Bear answered without hesitation, "I think I'll stay on here, Captain. Cedartown is beginning to seep into my blood and feel more and more like home." There, he did it!

Chapter 15

"Frenchie is in the cell again."

"Is he awake yet?"

"Don't know." Clara didn't look up from her typewriter. "I haven't checked.

"Don't disturb him. He'll be on his way soon." Bear picked The Cedartown Express up off her desk. "Anything I need to know?" He perused the headlines. "Jumper is losing it. His report about the body is merely factual." He threw down the paper. "He's probably preoccupied with an undertaking that appeals to him more, one that twists the soul of someone who is still around to suffer."

Clara answered, still not looking up from her typewriter. "The man is not liked."

"That is certainly true. He seems to be pleasured by stepping on as many toes as possible. I wonder what makes a man like that."

Clara pushed herself away from the desk. "Could be his size. He can't be 5 feet tall. Imagine what it must be like for him to have to spend his life always looking up at people."

"I suppose you're right but not all short people have a skunk's streak."

"True enough." The phone rang and Clara picked it up and listened without saying much. "She hung up and looked on the verge of tears."

"Who was that?"

"Mira, the telephone operator."

"Of course."

"Alice Mason called for an ambulance. They've taken David to the hospital. It's bad."

Bear fell into the chair opposite Clara and looked off into space. The theft of innocents: how does this world work? What are the Gods up to? What in hell is one supposed to learn from this tragedy? The sound of footsteps pulled him out of his reverie. He recognized the rhythm and weight of the pace. Before she appeared, he knew it was Elsa.

"You heard?" Clara asked.

Elsa pulled up another chair, nodded her head.

"Mira!" They said in unison.

"The news sent me over."

"What can we do for Alice Mason?"

"The whole town will be 'doing' for Alice. There'll be more food delivered to her house than she could eat in months. We all want to help. We'd better come up with some added ideas. Various things pop into my head but I throw them out before I close my palm over them." Clara went to the coffee machine and served up three mugs.

Their shared sympathy was a balm for their helplessness.

The door opened from the corridor housing the three cells and Frenchie staggered out smelling like the toilet of a brewery.

"Whew, Frenchie! I think a bath is in store for you."

"C'est vrais." He looked at the coffee machine yearningly.

Clara got up and poured another cup, handed it to Frenchie, who, aware of his fragrance, kept his distance by remaining leaning against the wall."

"Why do you keep at your job, Frenchie? "Elsa asked.

"Not other work for fat Frenchman, and the money, she is good."

"Where were you born, Frenchie?"

"In town in the North of Quebec. But I not like the people there and they not like me. So, I come to Cedartown twenty years ago and I still here."

"Your wife came with you." Elsa reminisced. "I remember her well. A petite woman very busy with activities at the Catholic Church."

"Oui!"

"Was she from the same town?"

"Oui. The town, it did not like my Dominique either."

"All of Cedartown was sorry when she died."

"C'est vrai. Everyone, they went to the funeral. It is a good town this: good people."

Bear wondered about the story beneath his conversation. Why did Frenchie and Dominique fall out of favor with a whole town? What did they do?

"We just heard they have taken little David Mason to the hospital. The iron lung must not have been doing its job. He's probably gone by now." Elsa choked on her words.

Frenchie grimaced in sympathetic pain. "Poor Mrs. Mason. I will clean her septic tank for her. They never hired me: it must need it."

He pushed himself away from the wall and, with a determined step headed for the door. They held their breath as he passed.

Clara fished out her perfumed handkerchief and sniffed. "At least he can help Alice in a positive way."

In the evening, on his way back to the boathouse, Bear stopped at the Farmers' Co-operative and spoke to Jack Ritter, the salesman behind the desk.

"Jack, can you tell me how many piglets George Brown ordered from you?"

"Evening, Bear. George had the original three delivered here. A Yorkshire, a Hampshire and a Duroc. Said once he knew what his customers wanted he would buy directly from the source." Jack leaned on the counter. "Is there a problem?"

"Nope, just checking. Thanks."

He could feel the salesman's questioning look rake his back as he left.

Chapter 16

Thanksgiving October 9th

The usual clientele were gathered for their morning brew. Bear took his regular seat beside Malcolm who was getting his morning entertainment through conversation with The Boys.

"Been busy Boys?"

"Can't say we have." George smiled, and leaned into his coffee cup.

"No more than most days." Speaker added.

"You're looking damned dapper."

"Well, you did invite us for Thanksgiving dinner."

"We did that, and Mrs. Fraser will be flattered that you've made an effort for her."

"Thought we might set an example for you, Sir," George teased.

The Captain laughed, flicked his ear and said, "You mean I'm not presentable?"

Bear wondered how George would respond.

"You, um-m-m, should we say are very talented at dressing down, Sir? Never seen expensive clothes worn so poorly." George sibilated. "And I'll tell you that for free."

Their continued back and forth. Teasing lightened all their moods. Even Elsa was laughing as she moved around behind the counter.

As they were about to leave, Jumper came in. They all went silent and turned away from him.

The little man cozied up between Bear and Malcolm, his head

not reaching their shoulders. They looked down at him as though at a stain that couldn't be removed. "I've been working on a project for The Legion," He smirked up at them. "They wanted photos of all the Cedartown men who died in the war. While I was at it I did a little more research as a gift for you" He handed Malcolm a large brown envelope. "Enjoy the memories Captain Fraser!" He retreated behind his camera and laughing, took a photo of Malcolm as he opened the envelope and peered in. "They're photos of all the Toronto boys from your battalion. The ones you left behind. I knew you'd be happy to have a memory of each one."

Malcolm stared at the photos one by one, going from one to another over, and over again. Without a word, he got up from his stool and, stiff-backed, left the restaurant. George and Speaker picked up Jumper from opposite sides and carried him out of the restaurant.

"Don't hurt him boys," Bear called. At least not when I'm a witness, he thought. Through the window he saw them speak to Jumper without changing their facial expressions insinuating a danger within the pair that was not normally visible. Jumper scuttled off but Bear didn't give the twerp much chance. Sooner or later the little jockey would receive his comeuppance.

The Boys stood on the sidewalk, stranded by fury. Bear got his hat and went out to them. He put his arm over the shoulder of each. They didn't turn. "I'll go after Malcolm."

"You'd best go quick, Bear. Those photos could be the end of him." George whispered. "A soldier needs to keep his agonies underfoot; stamped into the ground."

"Out of the cage they're a cancer," Speaker agreed. "You gotta keep them in their place."

The skies had opened up: booms of thunder followed spikes of lightening that cracked over the lake: too close for comfort. Bear ignored the downpour and jumped into his car. Where would Malcolm go? He drove to his house but the car was not there and he turned around in the driveway without getting out. No sense in upsetting Mrs. Fraser. On the beach-road there was no car. Where would he go? Into the woods with a gun? Bent over the wheel trying to see out the windshield through the pouring rain he drove all over Cedartown without any luck and finally went down to the harbour where Jack Winston was standing outside by his gas tank getting soaked to the skin. He gestured to Bear to get over there fast.

Bear slammed the car door and ran.

"That madman Fraser has gone out in his boat." Jack screamed through the downpour. "I yelled at him to stop but he ignored me."

"I'll have to go after him." Bear yelled.

"Don't be an idiot, Bear. The waves are three feet high."

Bear ignored him and ran into his boathouse, and started to lift the gate with the strap, when Speaker crashed through the door. "We'll take the Island Boat. It's bigger."

Bear released the pulley and the door banged down as they ran back to the Wawanesa, which George had running and ready.

As they jumped into the boat and started off Jack Winston's voice, muffled by the wind chased after them. "There's nothing you can do, you idiots. Come back."

The platform at the end of the pier was engulfed by waves. Bear knew they should turn around, but what of Malcolm? How could they leave the poor man out there? So, he held on and said nothing as they headed smack into monster waves capped in white foam that appeared like a threatening grimace: each attack trying to swallow them into the depths.

"She's a witch, this one." George held tight to the wheel. "She'll tear us apart if she can."

The Island boat had a wooden hood but the openings were without glass making them victims of furious wind which tore their lips from their chattering teeth. They were soaked to this skin with water dripping down their faces making it almost impossible to see.

"Look at the whitecaps on this lady, she's out for the kill, that's for sure." George's weak voice could not be heard over the tumult of the storm but Speaker and Bear knew what he was saying.

"We've never let a woman defeat us yet," Speaker yelled through the howling wind, "And she won't this time, but we'd best put on life preservers. Where the hell are they?"

"Somewhere in the hold." George couldn't look away from the lake nor release his grip on the wheel, and he couldn't yell.

Even holding on to the window frame Speaker and Bear were unable to keep erect. "I go down there and I'll be smashed to bits!"

"You don't go down and the lady may beat us this time".

Each time the boat climbed up over a wave and smacked down into a gully the effect sent pain shooting up through Bear's heals and spiraling through every bone in his body. Up, up they went, would the boat hold together with such jarring smacks? Each time Bear's head almost jerked off his neck. "How are we going to see anything in this storm?"

Speaker had crawled down to the hold, retrieved life preservers and thrown them up, following behind in a crawl.

"Keep an eye out for his boat." George screeched. "If we don't see anything between here and the island I'm afraid we'll have to pull into our harbour. "This is one mad lady."

Bear kept wiping the rain from his face and trying to see something out there on blinding maelstrom.

"Don't know how the hell we'll make it to our harbour." Speaker yelled.

"Shut up and keep looking." Bear insisted. He knew they'd have to turn around soon.

All conversation stopped, each man concentrating on his task: Speaker looking north and Bear south and west. George clung to the wheel. Bear looked back to the uncovered part of the boat and saw water had covered the floor; then realized it was up to his ankles where he stood. Each time it rose up and banged into a trough, it felt as though the old boat would rip apart: their silence was an acknowledgement of the danger they were in.

"What's that? Bear pointed at a black object dancing in the waves near the south end of the island.

All three tried to see through the furious wind and rain.

"It could be a boat." George said.

"We'd best see. If it's not Malcolm's we have little chance of finding anything else."

"I hope this rattletrap holds together long enough." Speaker yelled

"Don't fret," George answered, "You've got your life preserver on and we're close enough to the island. You'll live even if the boat dies."

Speaker and Bear leaned out the sides to try and see the object that was being tossed by the waves. "It is a boat, and there's a body in it."

Bear removed his life preserver, stripped off his pants, shirt, shoes and socks, then crawled to the back of the boat where he lifted the seat and grabbed a rope. Speaker followed on hands and knees. Bear tied the rope around his waist then anchored it down on a railing. "That boat is going to flip very soon. I'll try and get Malcolm out and you'll have to pull us in."

Speaker nodded and Bear jumped.

In the water, Malcolm's boat disappeared as Bear fell into a gully between waves. His strong stroke enabled him to fight his way over white caps, but it was exhausting: he'd better go under the waves. Beneath the surface the world disappeared: his thoughts slowed down and only with the greatest of efforts was he able to force himself up again. He was alone, one with the lake in a battle he was close to losing. The boat had not been far, why was it taking so long to get there? He closed his mind and kept going, finally coming up at the side of the boat. He pulled himself up on the edge but did not have the strength to climb in. Malcolm was lying across a seat, a spot of blood on his chest and a gun tossed around on the flooded floor.

There was no time to think or be gentle. He grabbed his friend by the hair and pulled him to the edge of the boat where he could get a grip under his arms then turned towards the big boat, and yelled "Pull!" before sinking under water with his burden. Speaker had heard! They were being yanked through the waves.

George was at the rope as well, and they dragged them to the side where Speaker leaned down and grabbed Malcolm while Bear sank in an effort to help push his friend up. He came to the surface coughing and spitting and had no strength left to climb in, but The Boys pulled him up, and he lay on the flooded bottom of the boat, unable to move. "Is he alive?"

"You check, Speaker," George ordered, "I've got to get back to the wheel. We've got problems."

They were being tossed around in the sloshing water making it almost impossible for Speaker to check on Malcolm. "I think there's a pulse. We'd best lift him on to a bench out of this water."

Bear forced himself to his feet and staggering in the heaving boat he and Speaker were finally able to lift Malcolm, who was unconscious, on to a bench. Bear tore open his shirt and saw a bullet hole just above the heart.

The boat rose higher, and higher and slammed down harder than ever creating a ripping sound in the bow. Bear had to hold on to Malcolm to prevent his being tossed over.

"That's it for this old crate," George croaked. "We'll never make it to our harbour. Only thing I can do is head for the closest shore, here on the south end of the island."

"There's no place to land the boat there." Speaker yelled.

"Nope, we'll crash on to Cass's beach if we're lucky."

Each wave created a squeal of wood. Bear tied his rope around Malcolm just in case they went down. Speaker pulled himself up to the helm to stand beside George and they waited as George fought the storm. "We'll make it." He sounded as though he was trying to convince himself. "Not far now."

"Hold on, I'm going to drive right onto the shore.

Bear, leaned over on top of Malcolm as the bottom of the boat screeched across the stone laden shore, and stopped dead, only to be rocked back and forth by the wind, waves, and rain.

"We'd best get out before she breaks up." George made his way to the open back holding on to the edges as he did so.

Speaker went over first and Bear and George handed down Malcolm then followed.

It was shallow enough to stand making it possible for them to battle their way on to shore. "Go ahead, George, and get Hawker to come and help." Speaker and Bear lifted Malcolm on to the beach.

"T'would be better if you went as I can't yell," and took over for Speaker.

"Get on with it Speaker." Bear yelled and started along the path carrying Malcolm.

The wind screeched through the trees, bending almost perpendicular. Pelting rain marred their vision, and fallen trees impeded their path.

With Malcolm in his arms Bear, with the help of George, managed to get over the first few, but were then faced with a huge trunk impossible to climb. Tears of effort ran down his already soaked face as he laid the inert body on the trunk. "Hold him, George. I'll go around. The tree was enormous, its branches as wide as a small room. He'd better go around the root. He slipped and slid through the mud and bush, being slapped by wiry stems too low and raw to be affected by the wind. The root of the overturned tree was twice his height and, with the earth clinging to it, was its own wall.

The storm had him in its clutches. He slipped and crawled and fell and stood and leaned and dragged himself around to the other side. George had his cheek pasted against the rough log, his hands still holding on to Malcolm's inert body. He looked up at the sound of Bear, his scruffy beard a waterfall riddled with bark. Bear leaned against the trunk took deep breaths and waited, face to the rain, for thought to return.

"Bear?" George leaned over the trunk and punched him on the back. "Snap to it. We have to move."

George's punch made him grunt and blink back to consciousness. "I'm not sure I can carry Malcolm any farther."

"You've got to. Now get with it." George hissed.

He slid Malcolm off the trunk and threw him over his shoulder fireman style. His knees bent with the weight and the body slipped. He grabbed one of Malcolm's arms and one leg to hold him in place and with muscles screaming straightened up and ploughed forward.

"Keep going, Bear, you're almost there." George encouraged. "I'll go around and be with you lickety-split."

Head down, Bear trudged forward trying hard not to slip, but the weight was too much for him and he felt himself going down on his knees forced to release one hand from his hold on Malcolm to prevent falling farther. He was frozen in place unable to stand and unwilling to collapse.

"I take him now." He heard Hawker say and felt the load being lifted from his shoulders.

George and Speaker grabbed Bear's arms and pulled him to his feet. Without words the three staggered behind the Hawker.

Cass was waiting at the door. "Put him on the kitchen table

Hawker." She followed and ripped his shirt open, saw the bullet wound and felt for his carotid artery. "There's still a pulse. We'll have to get those clothes off." She looked to the men for help. Bear had collapsed in a chair unsure he'd be able to move again—ever. The Boys appeared to be in a similar state. George's head had collapsed on his chest and Speaker was on the floor, leaning against the wall with his eyes shut. "We'll have to do it Hawker." Cass decided.

They achieved the task with surprising agility. Cass got a blanket, which she took to the sofa in the living room and ordered Hawker to carry Malcolm in, and she wrapped him up, put a pillow under his head and returned to the kitchen. "There's nothing I can do but keep him warm and pray." She surveyed the shivering men. "You two had better get out of your clothes," she said to Speaker and George, and turned to Bear, smiling. "And you'd better get into some." Bear didn't understand, until he looked down at his body and realized all he had on was a very soaked pair of undershorts. He was too tired to be embarrassed. "I'm not exactly equipped with men's clothes, but perhaps Hawker can come up with something."

There was no electricity: the wind was screeching around the house: rain pelted the windows, there was barely enough light to manoeuver, and the dogs were yelping the fear that they all felt. They pulled the sofa as close as possible to the fire that Hawker had going, and crowded in close to the warmth. Hawker boiled water on the flames and made a welcoming tea for them all.

Cass massaged Malcolm's arms, legs, shoulder and head trying to stimulate life into the prone body. They heard a moan and all of them surrounded Malcolm, whose eyes flickered.

"Malcolm?" Bear was on his knees beside his friend.

Malcolm opened his eyes. "Dead voices. Noise too much." He exhaled in a large whoosh and died.

Before Cass wrapped the blanket around his lifeless body Bear could see a relaxation of sinews: lolling head, released mouth, and eyelids closed over an absence of tension. The electricity was gone. Malcolm had finally escaped the noises in his head.

The three men stood over the body in silence. Tears rolled down

George's cheeks, Speaker screwed up his face and chewed his lips. "I'm going' to kill that god-damned, shitting fuck, Jumper!"

George shook his head. "T'was the war that did it. Malcolm did things no man was meant to do. He made it through the battle but came home diseased with memories. It's the good men that suffer most."

"Hawker, move Malcolm to the room upstairs." Cass whispered. "And then we'll find something to eat for you all."

"Better something to drink," George whispered.

"I have that too."

After Malcolm was carried off, Bear sat in the sofa where Malcolm had been lying and felt the indentations in the cushions. He rubbed his hand over where his head had been. What was it about taking one's own life that was unacceptable when using that same life to commit atrocities was acceptable? It was the death of others that had flung Malcolm into deep suffering.

"A lot of trees are down." George stared out the window and watched the storm.

"How long do you think it will last?" Bear remained on the sofa, still stiff from the exertions of the day before.

"Can't tell," George whispered. "Mother nature is one confusing bitch."

They sipped their drinks. The wind screamed at the windows, Trees split and cracked. They didn't talk.

"Sorry about the Wawanesa," Bear said.

"I'll miss her," George didn't turn from the window. "I'll get another, but it won't be the same; takes years to soften the luster and make her seaworthy.

"Do you have the money to buy another one?"

George nodded his head but didn't explain.

Bear chose not to ask. "Where are Speaker and Cass?

"In the kitchen. Talking about Cass's book."

Bear laughed. "It won't get him anywhere."

"No," George whispered, "But she'll be happy to tell him anything he wants to know and that's enough to get him excited. He'll have wet dreams for months."

George still hadn't turned away from the window

An overwhelmed laugh broke through Bear's lips. Here we are in the middle of a raging storm isolated in the house of a famous Madam, with no possible escape and unable to do a thing with the body of our friend. Malcolm would probably find the situation amusing. He bit back the ridiculous smile. There was nothing funny about now or about what was to come. He would have to tell Tess and Mrs. Fraser and little Essie. What should they do with the body? How would they get off the island? How long was this damned storm going to last?

"Jack Winston knows where we went."

It was as though Speaker had read his mind.

"Hell come after us soon as he can." Speaker went on. "Hope it's soon. It's kinda unsettling stuck here with Malcolm stiffening up."

"Couldn't agree with you more, Speaker."

Chapter 17

On the third day of the storm, after Malcolm's body had been moved to the barn, Cass called from the kitchen, "Georgie, come upstairs with me, will you? I want to talk to you alone."

Relieved to be pulled out of his moping, George pushed himself away from the window and followed Cass up the stairs. Once there, they embraced long, hard and silently. Words would ruin the pleasure.

"At least with this weather I don't have to worry about you being threatened" George said after they finally sat down.

"I think I've figured out how to deal with the threat." Cass leaned over to the desk and pulled a pile of paper on to her knee. "This is my manuscript."

"Finished already?"

She laughed, "I've been writing it for years. Just had to pull it all together." She handed it to him. "Will you have three copies made, and then send them to the addresses in Toronto that I'll give you, with covering letters for each?"

"This is not a good idea Cass! It's asking for trouble!"

She patted his knee. "No, no Georgie, this is the proof that I've not exposed anybody. It's not about crooks and corruption it's about just plain old sex." She laughed. "When they read it they'll know, and I'll include a letter saying that this is all I'm ever going to write." She patted the manuscript on his knee. "So will you do it for me Georgie?"

"You know I'll do anything for you, Cass," he whispered and took up the manuscript to have a look. The title was 'HOW TO HAVE A PLEASURABLE WHOOPEE by TORONTO'S MERRIEST MADAME.' He swallowed and turned to the table of contents.

'Chapter 1: ORGIASTIC PLEASURES, Chapter 2: TWADDLING THE CLITORIS, and dropped the whole thing back on his knee. "How the hell am I going to take this to a printer? I'll be arrested!"

"No you won't Georgie. You'll arouse curiosity but it won't hurt you," she laughed "And once I have this printed the wolves will be calmed. And, I might add, the shock of the thing is going to make it a best-seller."

"The wolves may be calmed, but what about the sex fiends?"

"That's why I'm here, where the shore's edge is rough and my best friend has the only island boat."

"Had."

"Oh, you'll get another soon enough, won't you?"

He couldn't argue with that and it wasn't the first time he had been forced to help Cass escape squabbles. From the time she was barely pubescent she'd created an adoring over-sexed group of men who wanted more and more of her and at whom she laughed. Often it was up to him to assuage their anger, he who was the only male never to have had sex with her. It sure as hell was a hard way to love a dame. "I'll go to Barrie and get it printed. They don't know me there."

"Thank you Georgie. I knew you would."

George riffled the pages, not sure that he ever wanted to read the damned thing.

"When you get your new boat and I get the wolves off my back, let's take a picnic to the flat rocks like we did as kids."

"That's a date." But he knew her better than she knew herself. As soon as she was out of danger she'd be off once more.

Close quarters in the midst of the storm initiated conversations that might not otherwise have ever taken place.

Bear poured himself a stiff drink from the bottle Cass had left on the table.

"You going to marry Elsa, Bear?" Speaker asked. "She's one special dame."

Bear threw himself down on the sofa. "Don't know, but I'm going to have to decide damned soon."

"What's to decide?" George asked in his croak.

"Whether to stay in Cedartown or not, Elsa will not move anywhere else."

"Can't say I blame her."

"She said she can hardly breathe when she's away from Cedartown!"

"This is her home, her air, her soil, her people. If she tried to give it up it wouldn't last" George added. "That I know."

"You going to leave us Bear?" Speaker was on his knees feeding the fire.

"I don't know. The Chief has offered a promotion but I said I'd let him know later. On the positive side is Elsa, on the negative, I'm not sure I want to continue being a cop"

"You're a good cop, Bear. You should stay. The town needs you."

"Thanks, I'm wavering in that direction." He suspected his roots were creeping under the pot-holed roads, but would he be able to serve the law if tested? Of this he was not a bit sure.

Hawker came in from outside. "The storm, it is dying."

Chapter 18

Jack Winston arrived at the door even before the storm had completely abated. "Couldn't wait any longer. Everyone is down at the dock worrying."

Hawker pulled him in. "De news, it is not good."

Winston came to an abrupt standstill when he saw the faces of the others. "The Captain?"

"Gone," George said.

Winston nodded. "Of course." He looked down at the blanket that enveloped Malcolm, whom they had returned to the house when they saw Winston had arrived. He pulled it away to see his face, and shook his head. "We have to get him back."

The path was mud, wet mud that sucked up every footstep and there were downed trees that had to be circumnavigated making the trek down to the lake with Malcolm's body tortuous. The blanket enfolding him became slippery: they almost dropped him.

"Open the blanket and we'll all four take a corner and get him down that way," Bear instructed. And with a stumbling struggle they finally made it to the dock where, with each wave, Winston's boat banged the bumpers hanging over the side of the dock.

Winston climbed in and struggled to keep his balance as he guided in the body which the four friends were gently handing down. He laid Malcolm along the floor and without looking up said, "There's only room for one other in this rattletrap."

Bear climbed down beside him. "It has to be me."

The others stood together on the dock and watched the small

outboard slam through big waves with Bear leaning over the body to keep it stable.

Cass put her arm around George and rested her head on his shoulder as they watched it disappear. Speaker crouched down on his haunches and shook his head over and over, and Hawker started back up to the house. "When de boat, it gets to de harbour, der will be tears wet with de suffering all mixed up with too many questions. Poor Mr. Bear."

Finally, the others turned to join him and were about to start up the path when George stopped and looked out over the lake. "I hear a boat."

They all looked across the lake. "There it is," Speaker said. "It's gotta be a big one coming all the way from Barrie in this weather."

"Hawker," George tried to call up the path and turned in frustration, "You call him, Speaker. Tell him to bring the guns."

As they watched the big boat becoming larger and larger as it approached, George whispered, "Hurry Hawker." And was relieved when the big man appeared before the boat closed in on the dock.

"Take the rifle into the trees and watch." George told Hawker and he took the pistol and pushed it into the back of his belt.

"Let's wait and see who it is, Georgie," Cass cautioned, "And give me a chance to deal with this with words."

"Words aren't often enough, Cass and I don't want you too close to whoever it is."

"You're wrong Georgie, words can massage better than threats. Let's give them a chance!"

The big boat approached slowly unsure of the water's depth. There was just one man standing at the wheel, and he waved.

"It's the Police Chief from Toronto!" Cass exclaimed. She smiled at George and rubbed his arm. "He's a friend, Georgie. It's alright." She went to the edge of the dock and waited while Speaker and Hawk accepted the ropes thrown out to them and tied them on the embedded rings.

"Chief!" Cass called, "This is a worrisome surprise."

Accepting Speaker's proffered hand, The Chief climbed out. He was a big, muscled man past middle age with the world imbedded in lines of his face. He was not smiling.

George hung back, still suspicious, still worried. He put his hand around his back to the gun in his belt. For Cass, he would even shoot the chief of police.

"We need to talk, Cass."

"Come up to the house and I'll give you something to warm you up and then we can talk."

Suitably refreshed the Chief stood up from in front of the fire and said. "We need to talk," he looked around at the men. "Alone."

"We'll go upstairs," Cass said. "I have something up there that you might want to see."

"I'm coming," George insisted.

"Alone!" the Chief insisted with the gruff sound of authority that lived deep in his voice.

"It's alright, Chief," Cass assured him. "George is my mate, my friend, my bodyguard, and the keeper of my secrets." And she started up the stairs presuming they would follow. And they did.

"Now," The Chief said as he sat in the chair by Cass's desk. "There are lot of important people in the city," he cleared his throat, "Myself included, that are very worried about the book you have said you will write. As an honest police chief, I -- "

"Not entirely," Cass interrupted with a smile.

He harrumphed. "As an almost entirely honest police chief I've been appointed to approach you and warn you that it is a dangerous undertaking, and that there are those in the city who would do almost anything to stop publication."

"Almost anything?"

"Not even 'almost'"

George could feel his anger seething and stepped forward ready to spout a threat himself.

Cass held up her arm to stop him.

"I'm quite sure this problem is easily solved, Chief." She opened the drawer and pulled out the manuscript. "George and I will leave you to have a look at this, and then we can talk afterwards." She tilted her head, smiled a naughty smile and beckoned to George. "Let's go down and join the others."

It wasn't long before they heard guffaws of laughter pouring down the stairs. It took quite a while before his big boots descended the stairs. "I'll take this to Toronto and have it published myself." He laughed. "It'll be a best seller, Cass. And a relief for a hell of a lot of your old 'friends',"

George will be relieved that you take on the chore of having it published won't you, George?"

"I could imagine myself growing a mustache and wearing sunglasses to preserve my reputation!" George smiled.

"I'll take care of it," The Chief answered, "with pleasure."

"And tell my 'friends' that I have no intention of furthering my writing career."

"They will be pleased. I'm also sure that none of them will admit ever having known you."

They all watched the Chief's boat disappear in the distance. "Now we have to figure out how to get out of here." George said still watching the boat as it diminished into a black speck.

"Jack Winston said he'll be back." Speaker said.

"Yes, but when? I can imagine what's going on at the harbour right now."

"One thing is for sure," Speaker said, "that little twerp Jumper will be in hiding."

"Don't be so sure," Cass said. "One of the great pleasures of evil men is to gloat."

"If he's even close with his camera, Bear will do something." George said.

"But not enough," Speaker stomped his foot and kicked at the dock's ladder. "Bear's a cop."

Chapter 19

By the time they reached the harbour both Jack Winston and Bear were soaked to the skin and Malcolm was almost floating in water. From the entrance, Bear could see a crowd gathered around the docking area. "Damn-nation!" he muttered. "Why so many people?"

"It's no wonder, Bear. For three days they have had no idea of what had happened."

"This is going to be awful!"

Jack slowed the engine as they approached. The group gathered there were immobile and silent. Bear saw through their eyes the realization that only two were in the boat and one was hunched over abnormally.

Clara and Elsa caught the proffered ropes and tied them. Bear stood up from his crouch revealing the blanketed body beneath him.

"Who is it, Bear?" Elsa was pale, her voice disturbed.

"Malcolm."

Elsa immediately pulled Mrs. Fraser into an all enfolding embrace but she was frozen in silence.

Jack Winston climbed out and said to Bear. "Best leave Malcolm where he is until an ambulance gets here." He climbed the two stairs to the landing. "I'll call."

Mrs. Fraser came down the steps. Bear embraced her and held her back from the body.

"What happened?" She whispered into his ear.

"He couldn't take it anymore, Mrs. Fraser."

Silence.

"He didn't drown?"

"No."

She pushed herself away and glared at Bear then turned to the sympathetic group. "Malcolm's boat overturned in the storm and he drowned." She didn't cry.

Surprised at the steel in her manner, Bear did not correct her, and looked up to see the ambulance arriving.

As they lifted Malcolm's body into the ambulance, a flash of the camera made everyone turn.

Electricity charged through his body. "You evil, unconscionable, half-pint of poison. I'll kill you with my bare hands!"

"No Bear! You'll do more damage to yourself than to him!" Elsa tried to hold him back but in his furor, he ignored her and she was dragged along helplessly.

Jack Winston stood in front of Bear and stopped him by slamming him in the chest with both hands "You're a cop Bear. Stop before you destroy yourself."

Bear shook his head back to conscious thought. "The man has to be stopped"

"I'll do it." Winston insisted. He turned and went after Jumper who was rushing to his car. When he caught up with him he tore the camera from the little man's neck, smashed it to the ground and stomped on it with his heavy boots, and didn't stop until the telescopic lens was flattened, film was eviscerated and the rest of the camera severely dented.

"This is an assault!" Jumper screeched. "Arrest him, Bear."

Bear just stared at him.

"I'll go to the provincials. There are witnesses. I know you all. I'll give them your names and we'll see!"

Every onlooker, one by one turned their back on him.

"You'll all be sorry," Jumper screamed. "I know your secrets." And he jumped into his car.

Bear turned back to see Mrs. Fraser getting into the car with Clara and felt guilty that he had lost control. He went over to her side window. "I'm sorry, Mrs. Fraser, what can I do?"

She shook her head. "I have to tell the children. I can't talk now. Later, Bear"

Chapter 20

Shepherding the coffin of a friend made the weight close to unbearable for George.

As they laid it down in front of the Presbyterian Church, he patted the wood. Don't know why you would want this, but here you are, Captain. He grimaced at the hypocrisy of the thing. The only reason the service was taking place at all was because Mrs. Fraser had insisted no one was to know that Malcolm had committed suicide. She had spoken quietly, but with determination. "He said he was 'a goddamned good christian' although he never went to church." With a faraway look, she added, "He would want a church service." And tears had moistened her eyes. "I wish you'd known him before the war."

He had engulfed her in a huge embrace surprising himself at his presumption. "We were all different before the war."

George returned to the pew and squeezed in beside Cass who had insisted on coming. "As much for you, Georgie, as for Malcolm," she had said. They held hands as Joe McPhee marched up the isle playing 'Amazing Grace' and she squeezed hard when the tears started rolling down his cheeks. The song made a huge moist bubble in his chest that could only escape through tears. He once was lost and now is found. George wished to God there had been another way for Malcolm, but knew the black beast that lurked in every soldier's shadow had escaped and enveloped him.

Cass knocked his shoulder and gestured with a tilt of her head to make him look over at the others sharing the pew. They were all crying; Elsa, Bear, Hawker and Clara. Even Speaker was chewing his lips to fight back the tears.

He ignored the hollow Christian words and concentrated on Malcolm. Before he knew it, he was carrying the coffin to the grave yard.

The friends stood close together as the coffin was dropped into the earth with a whoosh that sucked out all air, all life.

When it was over Elsa whispered to them all. "I've closed the restaurant. Come, after we speak to Mrs. Fraser, we'll celebrate Malcolm in our own way."

The mourners were all mingling outside the front of the church. Cass put her arm through George's. "We'd best chat up the gossip mongers. I have a feeling that no matter what they think of me they'd protect me from outsiders.' She smiled at him. "'Specially if I'm on your arm."

"Hope you're right," George croaked. "When your book comes out there'll be men hornier than a cat in heat."

"It's why I want them to think you and I are a pair, not to be interfered with."

"Are we?"

In answer Cass smiled and squeezed his arm.

In the Little Brown Jug, they all gathered around the U-shaped counter and Elsa served coffee after which she pulled out a bottle of rye from beneath the counter, and winked at Bear, "We're closed so it's ok."

They all waited for Bear's comment. To relieve the anxiety, he took the bottle and poured a glug into his coffee.

"I hear dat some men, they be chased by a huge black magic beast when dey get back from de war." Hawker looked at George. "C'est vrais?"

"Something like that," George croaked.

They sat in shared silence sipping their spiked coffee.

Elsa looked over her shoulder from the stove where she was preparing food to fill some part of their emptiness. "Cass, I'm glad you're here. It was brave of you to face the whole town at once."

Cass stared into her cup, took a deep breath and looked up. "I don't give a damn my dear. Hell, three days in my house on the island where we cried, laughed, were upset and even sometimes furious with each other, made these lugs my special friends." She smiled. "It's more than enough to make me ignore the opinions of others."

Clara, sitting as erect as she does in front of her typewriter, said, "Friendship is always a test, and being friends with a pair of marginal criminals, a retired trapper turned bodyguard, a famous Madam, a cop and a restaurant owner, will, I know, test me continually." Without a change of expression, she continued, "But you've all captured me and I am committed."

"Will Mrs. Fraser and the children be alright?" Eva asked.

Bear sipped his coffee. "I think so. "They're surrounded by family, right now, but when they all leave there will probably be a huge let-down. That's when we'll need to be attentive."

"I told Mrs. Fraser that if she wanted, I'd beat Jumper to a pulp," Speaker was monopolizing the bottle.

"Please God, you didn't?" Bear banged the top of his head with his hand.

"Why not? What's the matter with that?" Speaker looked bewildered.

George massaged his friend's shoulder. "Perhaps it wasn't the right moment,"

Speaker shrugged his shoulders and looked as though he didn't understand.

"What did Mrs. Fraser say?" Elsa asked.

"She was real nice. Just said 'thank you, Speaker, but it's not necessary." He picked up the bottle and shook out the final drops. "I might do it anyway: that little turd."

Bear had been mostly quiet. Strange that Malcolm's death has brought them together in friendship and separated them in their reactions. Not so unusual he supposed. He pushed away from the counter. "It's been a long, tough day. Thank you, Beautiful Elsa for feeding us, but most of this crew have to get back to the island, and Clara and I have a bit of paperwork before I collapse."

"Thanks for the use of your boat, Bear." George said

"Keep it until you get a new one." He gestured to Clara, "To work we must go."

It was late when Bear finally arrived at the boathouse. He could hardly keep his eyes open. A quick shower and to bed. He felt his eyes being pulled shut – emotion sure as hell weighed heavy.

Hardly remembering how he got there, he collapsed in bed and shut his eyes.

A noise brought him out of black sleep, but didn't waken him until it continued, bang, bang, bang. It was someone knocking on the door. What time was it? He staggered up and opened the door and Tess threw herself into his arms weeping and stuttering deep sobs.

He found himself with his arms around her before he was fully awake. Please God, this can't happen.

He untied her arms from around his waist and steered her to a chair. Her sobs were insurmountable, and added to the tragedy was a look of incomprehension. "I need you to hug me don't you understand?" she wailed.

"I'm sorry, Tess." What could he say?

"I loved Daddy so much! He loved me best."

"I'm sure he did."

"And now there's no one who loves me best."

He sat down in the chair opposite her and took her hands. "Who are you crying for Sweet Tess, yourself or your father?"

She jumped up from the chair so fast it tilted backwards and almost over and she stamped her foot. "For Daddy, who else?"

She looked so tempting with her little breasts almost shivering with insult and the tears flowing. "I'm sorry." Of course, she doesn't see it. Before he could go on she'd flung herself on top of him.

"Hug me Bear! Please!"

Again, he found himself with his arms around her fighting a battle between body and mind. "Of course I'll hug you Tess." He inhaled and continued. "You are a sweet little girl and it's going to be really tough to continue growing up without Malcolm." Bear held her tight and rubbed her back. She turned her tear-laden face up to him and, without thought, he leaned in to kiss her sensual pout. Before it happened there was a knock on the door, and Bear broke away. What was he thinking? He gently pushed the girl-child aside and went to the door.

George, was there looking down at the ground and scratching at the front of his hairline. "Thought, maybe I could take Tess home for you.

Embarrassed at the sight of his arousal, Bear turned away from George and replied in a husky voice, "That would be a good idea. Thanks, George." For saving me from myself. He took Tess's hand "I'll do everything I can for your family, Tess, but it's you they need now." He lifted her chin and dried her tears. You have to be strong for them." A hell of a lot stronger than I was in the last half hour. Thank God for George.

"But I want to stay here, with you," she wailed.

"That's not a good idea, Tess. I'll be over to visit your mother tomorrow." He pushed her into George's clutch and shut the door.

George stood in the middle of his mirrored room and saw himself looking over his own shoulder.

It was a good thing you burned your fatigues, Whispering George. It would have made starting all over impossible if you'd tried to put a new shirt on top.

You should have told the Captain that, and don't put your fists on your waist and shake your stupid head. You thought him too many rungs above you to be his friend. You could have helped and you didn't.

That man was a brave S.O.B. He weighed the consequences, was scared shitless, but did what was expected of him. I, and the others, were so indoctrinated, we didn't think, we just barged ahead. And the world said we were courageous. There's a big god damned difference between bravery and courage.

It's a sad face you're looking at, Georgie, and it hurts. Smarten up, Boy.

Unable to castigate himself any further he went out on to his porch and stared down at the lake. Wind was making white caps on the waves. A piece of wood was rising and falling but not moving. Water won't move it, only Wind will.

He felt his smile sneak back to the edges of his mouth. He guessed he'd saved Bear from calamity. He had been heading to Bear's boathouse to use his boat to get to the island when he saw the half-innocent coquette going in. Bear was a good man, he hoped to hell he wouldn't let his hormones ruin his life.

The leaves were beginning to fall. Winter would arrive soon, and along with it those few weeks when the ice was forming but was too mushy to either boat or walk the water. It had always been a time when the islanders closed in on themselves, sometimes incestuously but forcing them to acknowledge their roots. He hoped he'd spend the time with Cass.

Chapter 21

Bear and Clara's evening drink had become a ritual of gathered friends. Hawker often brought Cass over from the island or they came with George and Speaker in George's new boat. When she saw them arrive Elsa popped over as well.

"Where's Speaker?" Bear asked.

"Attending to his hormones," George dragged a chair from Bear's office.

"It's a month now since Malcolm died." Elsa said, "and I'm upset with myself that he comes to my mind less and less." She smiled a wan smile and looked around. "Am I alone in this?"

"You're not alone, Elsa," Bear looked around, "I'd guess we're all a little guilty.

George got up and wandered over to the window. "Last year I had to cut down my favorite maple tree that was disease-infested and rotten. When I remember it, I remember its glory days when its fall colors were the most vibrant on the island and it stood strong and proud, knowing it."

"It will be like dat with Mr. Malcolm too. Now he is up in de sky with de angels, we will have de good memory down here."

Hawker's comment made them all smile.

Clara's phone rang.

She picked it up and listened. "It's the hospital, Frenchie was in an accident." Clara held the phone away from her ear. "He wants to speak to you in private."

"I'll take it in my office." He sat behind his desk and lifted the receiver. "Doctor?"

"Bear, It's Andrew Morrison"

"Good to hear your voice, Andrew."

"I'm here in Orillia doing my turn in the emergency room. Frenchie was over here buying some equipment for his business, when he was hit by a car. He's in pretty bad shape with a lot of broken bones."

"Will he be alright?"

"With time, but that's not why I called you. There's a bigger problem here, and I think you and your friends will be better able to deal with it."

"Tell me."

"When we cut his stinking clothes off him we found the unexpected."

"What was that."

"You won't believe it Bear. Frenchie is a woman!"

Frozen with shock Bear had no response.

"And there's worse. Jumper chased the ambulance and I think he heard us all talking about it."

"Thanks Andrew. We'll be over to console him, I mean her, as soon as we can."

"She won't be out of surgery for a couple of hours yet. Tomorrow would be the earliest you could see him or her, or whatever."

Bear cradled the receiver, smiled and shook his head. "I'll be god-damned!"

In the outer office, they were all awaiting the news with worried countenances.

"What happened to him, Bear, is Frenchie ok?" Elsa asked.

Bear had difficulty lifting his gaze from the floor. "He was hit by a car and has multiple fractures. He's in surgery now, but the doctor says he'll recover."

"Poor man," Clara said in sympathy. "Ever since his wife died he's been knock down drunk almost every night and belligerent on Saturday nights." He's really a good person who's lost control." She squeezed her lips together. "I like the man."

Bear kneaded his cheek, unsure what expression he was to permit surface. "The thing is there's more – a lot more actually."

They looked at him expectantly.

"When they stripped him of his stinking clothes they made a discovery."

"What discovery?" Elsa insisted

The smile won the battle between expressions. "It turns out our friend Frenchie is a woman!"

Cass let out a loud guffaw and clapped her hands with pleasure. The others looked stunned.

"That's why he left his Quebec town. He/she was in love with a woman, and was probably found out." George surmised.

"And he," Elsa shook her head, "damn it, she, knew that not even Cedartown would understand."

"Shouldn't change things," George advised, 'Frenchie's still Frenchie."

"Oh, but what a wonderful deception," Cass laughed. "It tickles me pink!"

"There's more." Bear interrupted. "Jumper, probably knows. He apparently chased the ambulance and overheard the doctors."

"Does it matter if he prints it? Everyone will find out soon enough," Elsa wondered.

"It matters." George muttered. "It's one thing to have the news spread in whispers that hold laughter and affection in the same breath. In The Express it will be written up as an exposé."

Clara rose to her feet, "I'm going to the hospital to be there when Frenchie wakens. She needs to know she has friends."

Elsa grabbed her coat from the back of her chair. "I'll go with you."

"I'll go and see if I can stop Jumper," George, too, headed for the door.

"You need the muscle of a Frenchman, Mr., George?"

"Thanks, no, Hawker. It's late. You'd best take Cass back to the island."

"Georgie's right." Cass pulled Hawker by the arm. "Let us know what happens."

Jumper lived in an apartment above the Five and Dime Store, a building that had seen better days. Its backside was one of those along Main Street that was slipping towards the river as its's banks eroded.

George had never been in Jumper's apartment but the moment called for severe measures. He climbed the side stairs, knocked on the door, and waited but there was no answer. Jumper had, apparently, not yet returned from his latest foray into collecting misery he could divulge in the paper.

Bubbling anger was percolating through his innards. Something had to be done about the little man.

He tried the handle but it was locked. Furious, he kicked the rotten door so hard it shattered the wood permitting him to reach in and turn the lock. He would go in and wait for the little twerp. What he could do to stop him from publishing yet another exposé he wasn't sure, but he sure as hell had to try.

Inside, there was a living room with horsehair drooping from the sofa cushions, empty beer bottles on the floor and table, photography magazines, some open others with mauled corners, scattered around the one big chair. In the kitchen, beside the sink was a stool for the little man and in the basin, a pile of dirty dishes.

The big closet in the bedroom had to be his dark room. Might be something in there he could use to hold against him.

Hanging on the development string were photos of little girls, all naked. They were in the changing room at the pier. He must have had a hidden camera. There was little Essie, pulling her shirt off, and the others, all Cedartown children. Vomit rose in his throat. He pulled down a couple. He picked up a wastepaper basket and filled it with every photo he could find. He'd take them directly to Bear. This will be the end of the little runt.

Just as he was about to leave Jumper arrived. "What the hell are you doing in my house?" He lifted the camera and took a photo of the door and then of George. "Breaking and entering." He laughed, his high squeaky laugh. "Not only is it a good story but I can charge you."

Seething, George's voice almost left him completely. "We'll see who charges whom, you little pisspot. I'm taking these directly to Bear, and if you dare publish anything between now and the time we're back, I, personally will murder you."

Jumper tried to grab the photos from George who held the container high above the little jockey's reach. "Those are mine you bastard! You have no right!

George pushed him so hard he fell to the floor and banged his head. "Right this minute I am having difficulty not pummelling you to death." He left before he committed a crime himself.

It was late, Elsa was in Orillia with Clara so Bear would be in his own bed tonight. George got in his truck and drove directly there.

Bear was asleep when George barged in without knocking, collapsed in a chair and flung the photos on the table.

Shocked at the noise Bear sat up quickly. Still in his underwear, jumped out of bed. "What?"

George pointed at the table and the photographs. Bear picked them up, looked at them, one at a time, then dropped them back on the table and stared back at George. "Do you think he was doing it for his own pleasure or was he selling them?"

"Don't know."

"It will make a difference with the charge," He grabbed his pants and jacket and wrapped his gun belt around his waist. "I'll arrest him now and worry about the charges in the morning." He stopped at the door. "I remember a day a few months ago when little Essie was holed up in the bedroom with cries that verged on hysteria. I hope it wasn't related to this."

Bear pulled the cruiser up in front of the Five and Dime and climbed the stairs. The damaged door of Jumper's apartment was wide open, and Bear knew immediately that Jumper was gone. He went in directly to the dark room. It had been stripped bare. Not a photo to be seen.

CHAPTER 22

Bear found Mrs. Fraser out in the garden clipping the last of the bright fall leaves off the maple. When she saw Bear, she gathered her bunch and walked to him holding up her collection. "The last vestiges of fall." She caressed a leaf. "It makes them more beautiful than the earlier ones. A final flourish before the end, I suppose."

"Could we have a chat Mrs. Fraser?"

"Goodness! There's no music in your voice today. What's happened now?"

"Nothing, I hope. But perhaps we should go in the house and sit down."

"Of course." She led him to the screened porch overlooking the lake. The wind fluffed her hair into angel wisps.

"Are the children at home?" Bear asked over her shoulder.

"Tess and John are back in school in the city. It was time." She stopped and turned around holding her branches between them. "Grieving shouldn't be coddled for too long, don't you think?" Without expecting an answer, she continued to the house.

Bear was relieved Tess was gone. "And Essie. Is she here?"

"She's somewhere around. I'm not quite sure where." She looked back and forth as though Essie might pop out of nowhere. "Give me a minute to put these in water. Is there anything I can get you?"

"No thank you."

She came back carrying a large vase holding the spray of fall, and placed it on a table. "Goodness! You do sound serious."

She sat down, folded her hands, tilted her head and smiled her ethereal smile. "Now, tell me what makes your eyes dance away from me?"

Bear handed her the brown envelope holding the photos, and watched her go through them one by one.

"I suspected something like this."

"What made you suspicious?"

"Essie talked continually about how Mr. Jumper was going to put their photos in a famous magazine, and I'd seen him down at the waterfront hovering around the wee ones, but it seemed quite innocent, really."

"Why was Essie crying so hard the day I came looking for Malcolm? It sounded as though her world had shattered, and Tess said you wouldn't open the door for anyone."

"That was serious for Little Essie, but it had nothing to do with those photos."

"Could you tell me about it?

"Oh, well, Essie was in the fairgrounds with her wagon picking up pop bottles left around after the baseball game. She often did that to collect the 2 cents she got for each bottle. That day a very drunk hobo staggered out of the barn and told her to reach in his pocket for the nickel he had there for her." Mrs. Fraser smiled. "She's a little business woman, that one." And then drifted into another world.

"What happened with the hobo?" Bear asked to bring her back.

"She reached into his pocket and all she found was his um-m-m, his organ in full flower. The poor child had no idea what it was but quickly withdrew her hand, and when the hobo tried to pull her into an embrace, she hit him hard with the soda bottle she had in her hand, and ran away."

"I can understand how upset she might have been."

"Oh, she would have dealt with that. The thing was, she thought she'd killed him."

"Why didn't you come to me, Mrs. Fraser, or at the very least tell Malcolm?"

"I took care of it myself, Bear. As soon as I got the whole story out of her and she'd stopped crying I drove over to the fairgrounds to look for the miscreant, but he was gone, so he was not dead and all was well."

Bear shook his head and watched her go through the photos once more seemingly having forgotten the story of Essie and the hobo.

She looked up from the photos in her hands, "There is so much beauty in innocence, and he did capture it well."

"Doesn't it make you angry at Jumper?"

"Not really, not this time." She looked over his head. "He didn't cause any harm to the little girls. The person he did harm to was Malcolm and that makes me very sad."

"Not angry?"

"Deprived. And yes, angry, too, I suppose, but I knew that he had cut the stitch on a very weak seam."

What world did this woman live in? "I'd like to speak to Essie if she's around."

"You might look for her outside, the child spends all her time playing in her own dream world."

Bear bit back a comment and left, forgetting to control the screen door as it banged shut. He found Essie in the front, climbing the crab-apple tree. "Hey Essie, that's a mighty climb for a little girl."

"I'm not so little any more Mr. Bear." She swung herself down with the ease of a little monkey. "I'm eight years old and next summer I'll be a Junior Red Cross Swimmer!"

"Passed the Tadpole class?

"Yup, and I have a badge Mom will sew on my bathing suit."

"Aren't you young to be a Junior Red Cross Swimmer?"

She twirled in a circle and hardly concentrating on their conversation. "That's what makes it special!"

Bear took her hand and shook it. "I am very impressed Miss Essie Fraser."

Only an eight-year-old could reward him with such an uninhibited smile.

He offered his hand. "Let's go and sit on the step. I'd like to ask you something."

They settled on to the step. Essie stared up at him with pleased expectations. "Can you tell me about the man at the fairgrounds.""

Her face fell and she turned away. "I don't want to talk about that."

"Alright Essie." He put his arm around her shoulder. I have just one question. What was he wearing?"

She frowned, "Clothes, of course, pants and a shirt."

"What colour was his shirt?"

"Kind of a splattered mud colour."

That was it! He gave her a hug. "Thanks My Special Friend."

"OK.," She answered in voice that suggested it was not ok and immediately escaped Bear and the step ran back to her tree to resume the delayed dream.

Chapter 23

George peeked into the hospital room. Elsa and Clara were on either side of Frenchie's bed. He tiptoed in and leaned against the window, away from the bed.

"It's a face we've never met," Elsa whispered as she stared down at the round cheeks, and full lips.

"How could we have not known?" Clara sounded angry at herself.

"The shit covered him." George explained.

"You mean her," Elsa corrected.

George shook his head in self-correction. "And the stink kept us all from getting too close to her." He smiled, "A perfect disguise," he said with admiration.

They all stared down at the familiar, yet unknown face. And she lay there without opening her eyes.

"Wait!" Her eyelids are dancing! You can hear us, Frenchie, can't you?"

"Leave her, George. She doesn't want to talk to us."

"She'll have to face the world sometime." He went to the edge of the bed. "C'mon, Frenchie," he whispered in has gravelly voice. "We're your friends. "Open up! "He pinched her cheek,

"Don't George." Elsa pushed his hand away.

Frenchie's eyes had popped open. She tried to turn her head away from them. Tears crept down her cheeks.

George cupped her chin and turned it back, and said gently, "Either you borrow my gun and shoot yourself or face it and let us figure out how to deal with it."

"We're friends, Frenchie, we want to help," Clara stroked the blanket covering the injured woman.

"Hell, we even liked you when you oozed toilet stink." George smiled.

"And even when you used our jail cell as your own personal hotel," Clara attempted to amuse.

Frenchie moaned.

"Are you in pain?" Elsa asked. "Is it terrible?"

"The pain in the bones, it is not so bad beside the pain of being undressed. Now the world, it will know about my sin: the church it will excommunicate me: Bear, he will have to arrest me." Sobs burst out from deep in her belly.

George put his hands on his hips and demanded with an anger that hurt his throat, "You're a sinner because you're not what the shit-scared rulers say you should be?"

"I know I'm not normal," Frenchie wailed. "But I can't help what I am!"

George stomped to the window. "Normal is as normal is, and no god-damned superior being can change it!"

"It's in the bible!"

"'Course it is! What would any religion want with homosexuals? It'd cut down on procreating followers!" George was surprised at his own anger. "They make their laws to protect themselves. They sure as shit don't want any pretty men or bull women to mix the flavor of their world!"

"Watch your words, George," Elsa warned.

But George's anger wouldn't stop. "You're as normal as they are, Frenchie." He looked around the room not sure where to put himself. "You're just different. It's a god-awful word—normal."

"Cedartown, it has become my home. Now I will have to go!"

"No you won't," Elsa said angrily. "We'll help you, you can come and work at the Brown Jug."

"Give your home a chance!" Clara's gentle smile softened the severity in her voice.

"It won't be easy," George warned. "Most in the world have to be directed on how to think." He headed to the door. "But winning a battle leaves a very sweet taste and I'll tell you that for free"

"But Jumper, he will expose me!"

Before leaving George turned his head. "Jumper is gone."

"It's taking longer than expected for Frenchie to get back on her feet" Elsa poured George his cup of coffee.

"Can't blame the poor woman," George said.

Bear did not join in. His silence hung heavy.

Elsa, who had taken out vegetables in preparation for the afternoon lunch, looked up from her work, "You're not going to arrest her, Bear!" She banged a knife on the table. "You can't!"

Bear shook his head. "Don't think I'll have to. There is a statute of limitations." He grimaced, "But even if I don't it's going to be hell, with demands for her head."

"It's nothing in comparison to what she's about to go through."

Clara, who never bent her body over the counter added, "There will be violent reactions, I fear."

"'Course there will be. George mumbled. "We just have to look inside ourselves to see we aren't so pure: the little demon of prejudice lurks inside us all."

Everyone was quiet. George hadn't meant to shut them all up.

Cass massaged George's arm. "If it doesn't work, I know people in the city, people like Frenchie, who have their own little society. I could introduce her. She may be happier there."

"Don't think so."

"Why, Georgie?"

"This is home."

"We must all be here on her first day," Clara decided. "She'll need all the support she can get."

On the day Frenchie had healed and was ready to start, the friends were all gathered outside the Little Brown Jug before it opened. With a worried expression, Elsa unlocked the door for them and locked it behind them. She gestured with her head to Frenchie who was collapsed over the counter with her head in her hands. "It is impossible! I cannot do this!"

"You have to choose between the being tough or being eaten up by the world." George mumbled. "Look at it this way: they'll only be preaching what they've been taught."

Frenchie pushed herself from the counter, wiped her tears and began to help Elsa with food preparations.

As soon as Elsa lifted the blind and opened the door, the good citizens filled the place acting as though it was just another day, but you could feel their curiosity and see smirks pass between friends.

Frenchie worked over the stove keeping her back to the customers.

Orders were made in quiet voices while every set of eyes was pasted to Frenchie's back.

"Welcome to the new world, Frenchie." This from Alice who knew suffering having lost her son to polio, and her husband in prison.

Frenchie turned with a nervous smile, which was quickly smothered at the sight of disapproving faces.

"You should be ashamed of yourself. You are a wicked sinner!" This from the fat lady in the hat.

"Go back into the shit where you belong!"

"Your life is a crime against Christ!"

"You're homier than a pet coon. Better that you disguise it with shit."

Frenchie stood frozen.

George could feel the seeds of hysteria mounting. He rose from his stool, "That's it!" but his fractured voice didn't carry.

But Frenchie held up her hand to stop him from going on. Her face hardened. She put her hands on the counter and leaned into the crowd. "Go ahead! Say what you think. I can't stop you. I am who I am, and you can't stop that."

"But I don't want her cooking my food," someone whispered.

"Then go elsewhere!" Elsa growled.

"We'll boycott your restaurant, Elsa, be careful what you decide." The speaker got up from his seat and spoke to the crowd. "Let's get out of here."

Some of the customers followed, but not many.

Children watched wide-eyed, and as soon as the seats were vacant climbed up on the stools and ordered ice cream sodas, uninterested in the drama of the thing.

Those who remained went on with their meals as though nothing had happened.

Chapter 24

"Where's Frenchie," Cass asked.

"She's at home," Elsa answered as she wiped the counter. "I'm afraid it's all been too much for her."

George watched Bear turning his spoon over and over and staring at nothing. His mercury sure as hell was low.

"Maybe it would be better if she - - -" Cass stopped when the Little Brown Jug's door was flung open so fast, the blind and the sign rattled and the door banged against the wall.

"Bear, "Clara called from the doorway. "You'd better get over to the office, there's a whole contingent of complainers waiting for you."

Bear climbed out of his reverie, "What do they want?"

Clara minced her lips, "Frenchie's hide."

"I've been waiting for this," he put his hat on and started out.

"So've I, "George whispered and joined him, with Cass and Speaker following fight behind.

Elsa took her apron off, "I'm coming too."

George, Speaker, and the others fenced the periphery of the crowd and watched Bear push his way through twenty cackling complainers.

When he reached his desk, he turned and gestured for silence with palms aggressively pushed at the voices. It worked. "Now, one at a time, please."

The mayor, a tall gaunt, mustachioed man started in a practical tone:

"Frenchie is a disturbance in this town as you can see, Bear. I think it would be best if you order her to leave."

"LEAVE? Not on your life! Arrest the bitch." This from the big bull-headed snow plow driver.

The Presbyterian minister, a small, fidgety man screeched, "You must not lie down with a male, the same way you lie down with a woman. It is a detestable act! Leviticus 18:22"

"What's that got to do with anything?" Speaker yelled. "Ain't no man in this conversation!"

"Flee from sexual immorality" the Anglican minister boomed. "Every other sin that a man might commit is outside his body but whoever practices sexual immorality is sinning against his own body. 1 Corinthians!"

Not to be outdone the United Church minister joined the rising hysteria. "But I see in my body another law warring against the law of my mind and leading me captive to sin's law. Romans 7.23

"What is this?" Speaker called out. "Bible study?"

Bob McTavish, who had hated Bear since the phone lines on his property were stolen, yelled, "It's buggery! Throw her in jail!"

"Buggers fornicate with sheep!"

The furor in Speaker's voice, surprised George.

"At least, Bear," the mayor yelled over the mounting noise, "She should be tested with the Fruit Machine to make sure she isn't continuing with her wayward ways!

Speaker looked at George with a frown, and whispered, "Fruit Machine? What's he talking about?"

"I'll tell you later."

"She didn't confess!" the Catholic priest moaned.

George looked at Cass and rolled his eyes. Cass looked angry.

"The law says homosexual men are criminal sexual psychopaths and dangerous sexual offenders deserving prison." This from the town lawyer.

"Not once, is a woman mentioned in all your god damned proclamations!" Cass called.

"Well listen here!" Bob McTavish bellowed, "Now it's an old whore telling us we're wrong!"

"ENOUGH! Bear banged his hands on the desk demanding and receiving silence. "I am not going to arrest Frenchie. Frenchie's companion died many years ago. Even if the laws of the nation do apply to her, there's a statute of limitations which would prevent her being charged." He collapsed in his chair spoke gently. "Now I want you all to go home and think about what it is in you that makes you so vociferous against a woman who loved another woman all her life. And I don't want to hear about this again!"

"Good for you, Bear", George silently congratulated him.

"And The Fruit Machine?" The mayor asked as he left.

With the complainers gone they all pulled up chairs around Bear's desk and Clara passed around rye in a paper cup. "We all need this, Bear, especially you, so no comment, please."

"Right now, I'm not capable of even a nice remark," Bear smiled a sad smile, "Make mine strong, dear Clara, please."

"What the hell's a Fruit Machine," Speaker asked.

"It's probably something I should know, but I have no god damned idea," Bear said into his cup.

"They use it in the army to weed out homosexuals," George said. "The Captain told me about it when he was laughing at the foolhardiness of the army. Apparently, the subject is put in a chair that's like a dentist's chair and forced to view pornography. While this goes on the device measures the pupils of the eyes and the pulse for a reaction that is contrary to the norm. And if the poor son-of-a-bitch reacts badly he's kicked out of the army!"

"Sounds idiotic!" Clara said.

"It may be but the army believed in it."

"Why?" Speaker wondered.

"Power? Fear? Who knows?"

Bear collapsed on the stool next to his regular stool.

"Looks like you've been ousted from your place." Speaker joked.

Pulled out of his exhausted reverie, "True, but by a beautiful dame." Bear smiled at Cass.

"Bet if you hadn't been ousted, you'd never have changed." Speaker frowned as he said this. "How's the view from the new stool?"

"The angle's a touch different." Bear retreated from the lightness back to the pack of worries he had to deal with.

The friends recognized his need for silence and waited.

"Someone threw a brick through Frenchie's window. It was wrapped in a paper that threated her if she didn't leave." With his elbow on the counter he rubbed his forehead. "People drive by her house and scream vitriolic insults: day and night." He looked up at Elsa," Where is she, by the way."

"Upstairs in my apartment." Elsa bit her upper lip. "She's leaving."

"Not surprised," George whispered.

"It's my fault!" Bear moaned. "I couldn't control the hate. It was like stepping on a cow pad. You quash the middle and it seeps out the sides."

"Where's she going?" Cass asked. "I could hook her up in the city with people like her."

"You don't get it, Cass," Elsa insisted. "That's not what makes Frenchie. It happened that she loved a woman and it has destroyed her life. She's a good woman, a good Catholic and a person who had the strength to love." Elsa crossed her arms and continued angrily. "All she wanted, was to be accepted—that Cedartown would become home as home is."

"We have to get her to stay!"

They all looked at Speaker with surprise.

"What?" he demanded.

"Just a little surprised at your vehemence, Cousin."

"Ah Hell! I saw it all when I was in prison. Elsa's, right, it ain't that important. What's important is that if she leaves it will be because she was ripped away and that's a hurt that never is forgotten."

"She's upstairs." Elsa took away their coffee cups.

They all trooped into Elsa's living room where Frenchie was sitting collapsed in the easy chair. Three suitcases were lined up in the middle of the room. They stood around awkwardly, until George sat on one of the suitcases and leaned into Frenchie. "We don't want you to go."

Tears moistened her eyes.

"I am sad to leave. But I am learning that friends like you," and tears rolled down her cheeks, "are not enough to fight the hate." Her voice stuttered with emotion. "You are too few. You cannot win."

George remained on the suitcase and the others found places on the sofa, except for Speaker who paced.

"You hid yourself in the shit, didn't you?" Speaker's voice was surprisingly gentle. "You thought you deserved it?"

"I did deserve it!" She answered. "My love, it was a sin against God and the church!"

"That's a lot of crap!" Speaker insisted.

With elbows on his knee and hands clutched in front of him, Bear said, "I'm sorry I couldn't do more." He looked down to hide his emotion but lifted his eyes to Frenchie. "I can't grab hate and throw it in prison."

Frenchie attempted a consoling smile.

"Where will you go?" Cass asked.

"Back to where I began. It is my only chance. Back to the smells I know." She pushed herself out of the chair. "I will return to the beginning. They will take me now that my Maria is not here. They will pretend it never happened." She tried to pick up a suitcase, but the men took them. "And now I am wise. I will know that there is a germ in the blood that needs very little help to bring sickness."

"We've all got some germ," George consoled

"It's time. George, will you take me to the station." The men who held suitcases put them down to embrace her in a farewell hug, and the others pulled her to them.

"We'll all go," Speaker insisted.

"Please don't," Frenchie asked. "This is a better place to say goodbye, I do not want an audience to my emotions."

"Damn!" Speaker gave her a second hug and turned away.

George thought there were tears in the eyes of his cousin who never cried.

At the station, before he unloaded the car, he turned to Frenchie. "In the hospital, Jumper got to you before your friends, didn't he?"

Frenchie looked frightened. "I think there was a flash of the camera. I was not all awake. He had the blanket down and my gown up. But when I woke up he was not in the room." She rubbed her eyes as though to rid herself of the vision. "I believed it was in my imagination. I told myself it was possible to dream such a dream about that evil man." Her eyes were wide. "I was wrong? There are photographs?"

"There were, I got rid of them. Nobody saw them, not even Bear."

"It is of no matter now," Frenchie lifted the handle to get out. "My story, it is neutralized."

As he watched the train carry off a good woman, he felt a heavy cloud of disappointment start in his head, press behind his eyes and rest the huge weight on his chest. It was a sensation he knew he would never be able to be completely free of. There would, he knew, always be a touch of evil wherever one lived, but the realization that ignorance nourished by the bible could tarnish his home so badly destroyed a deep comfort that he knew would never fully return.

Chapter 25

It was the 'soft time' when the ice was new and soft and travels to and from the mainland were impossible. George was in Cass's kitchen making chaga, a tea from the fungus that grew on the bark of the birch tree, which he'd dried, and cut up and was now boiling into a tea.

Cass peeked over his shoulder. "I'd forgotten about chaga."

"How could you? It cures everything, prevents infection, keeps you healthy, fights the common cold, prevents cancer, and a lady I know says it helps with bedroom problems!" He continued to cut his dried chaga into manageable junks, and looked over his shoulder with a devilish smile. "This, my gal, is the beginning of a new business. I'm going to sell it on the mainland."

"Probably a good idea. One of these days the town council will get rid of the liquor laws." She put her arms around him. "You'll have to close down your still."

He smiled without turning his head, "That's true, but until then, I'll carry both in the same kind of bottles and if the provincials come after my boat, I'll pull out the chaga that I've tinted with apple juice." He turned, put his arms around her and spun. "And I'll convince customers that a drink a day is an absolute necessity

Cass threw back her head and laughed.

Together they collapsed on the sofa, a stared out at the lake, enjoying a comfortable silence,

"The book's probably out by now." Cass's voice couldn't hide the excitement in her voice.

"Could be it's a good thing it's the soft time."

She looked at him with a half-smile. "You mean because I'm going to be infamous?

"Umm-hmm. And I have you to myself. "You have a month before your whole world changes". He put his arm around her shoulders and pulled her to him. Without looking at her he asked. "When you wrote the book you mixed your future with the ink and you knew that. So, what's your plan? What're you going to do with your unsavory fame, Cass?"

She punched him gently on the arm. "I'm going to ride its wave and squeeze as much money as possible out of it, and then come home." She put her head on his shoulder. "Fame, has a faulty wick. Soon I'll be nothing but the old whore living out on the island."

"And you'll stay then?" He tried to sound practical. But the yearning sneaked through.

She stood up, took his hand and pulled him into an embrace. "Yes, then I'll stay, so I think it's time."

Knowing exactly what she meant, he stood away from her and stared into her eyes. "Time for me and not another man—ever?"

Cass smiled a teasing smile. "Is that a prerequisite, Georgie?"

He didn't return her smile. "Afraid so, my girl. Don't want you till I can have all of you." He kissed her gently on the lips.

"Perhaps we'd better wait then," She joked, but he could tell she was hurt.

"Look Cass, I've loved you since we were kids, and wanted you since my first wet dream, but I've waited a long, long time for the moment when I will never have to share you. If it happened it would kill me."

She pushed him away and stomped into the kitchen. "Do you think I don't know that? She grabbed a wet cloth and flung it at him. "When I said it was time, that's what I meant!" She started banging pots on the counter, and when that didn't assuage her anger she threw them on the floor. "But inside that damned head of yours is a little kernel of disbelief. You're as bad as the crowd that attacked Frenchie!" Angry tears rolled down her cheeks. "And it hurts like hell!"

There was the truth in her words. He had witnessed Cass's whoring for so long, the kernel had sprouted. He had not believed her. He was wrong. He went to the kitchen and embraced her flailing arms and kissed her with all the passion he had held back forever.

They broke apart, smiled crooked smiles at each other and went to the bedroom.

"Great Zeus!" There was a crack in George's whisper.

"It was perfect, Georgie, better than anything ever!"

He gently smoothed her lips with his fingers, "Sh-h-h!" And fell back on the bed. Outside the window the ice was beginning overwhelm the water. Go slower, George begged the attacking blocks.

"You should move in." Cass put her head on his chest.

"Can't!"

She looked up at him, surprise on her face, "Why not?'

"My boat's at the harbour. Nowhere to dock it here." He smiled over her head. "And I need my mirrored room."

"We could make one here for you."

"A room maybe but not a harbour. "We'll work it out, but let's get you through your year of fame first." He put his feet on the cold floor. "I'll get some wood for the fire."

She got up on her knees and kissed his back. "And I'll make some hot toddies." Her voice had music he'd never heard before.

"With rum!"

"Of course."

Outside, George loaded his arms with wood from the pile under the lean-to. The loss of yearning left him somewhat empty. Cass was his now. It was a bit like winning the lottery and not knowing what the hell to do with it. Was Cass more confident? Did she not wonder about her commitment? Would she waver when she received all the attention of the outside world?

Ah hell! Forget it Georgie. Enjoy every minute of it. Don't just prune the doubts, pull them out!

Chapter 26

1951

Ice huts, plunked into the silence of the dead-still snow. dotted the three-mile expanse between Cedartown and the island,

There were too many huts set over the deep part of the lake where the trout could be found. Billie Wilkenson decided he'd place his hut over the shoal close to shore and go after whitefish. With ice creepers attached to his boots, he harnessed himself to his large sleigh that held the hut and necessary equipment.

At his chosen spot, he pulled the small cedar hut off the sleigh and mounded the edges with snow. He managed the undertaking with ease and little thought. Next, he retrieved the coal stove and shoved it through the small door and to the back where the stove pipe on the remade milk can could be connected to the exit on the roof. That accomplished, he hammered the bracket of the coal oil lamp on the wall and returned to the sleigh for the rest of his equipment.

Back inside he doubled the burlap bag filled with straw which the fishermen called 'donkey's breakfast', and knelt on it with his new ice chisel in his hand. Well away from the stove he carved out a three-foot circle in the ice. Damned if it wasn't like cutting through butter with the new-fangled gadget. He should go back for coal but first, one try. He grabbed his new cedar jigging stick wrapped with line and capped with the brass tip of a shotgun shell. To the end of the line he tied a snagger hook with three prongs spread out like a star. In the center, he secured a salted minnow, then, still on his knees lowered the homemade apparatus into the hole and smiled. The water in the hole was crystal blue. He stared, unblinking, at the pull of the deep.

There is a special talent amongst men, one which women envy, that being the ability to blank out the world, like whiteout on words, and find an, at least temporary, release. Billie Wilkinson was there, in that place, moving his fishing line in a hypnotic wave.

The snagger hit the bottom: not where the whitefish would find it. And then it stuck! He stood bent over the hole and pulled back and forth from different angles. It wasn't a fish, it was something heavy, a big stick or a log. He would have to pull it up and hope to be able to grab it through the hole. Finally, it bumped against the ice and he could see it. With a shocked reflex, he dropped it right back down into the lake, cut the still-attached line, tied it to the hook on the wall and, forgetting to put on his ice creepers, ran as fast as he could manage over the lake, slipping and falling in his rush, but not stopping until he reached Jack Winston at the boathouse.

George, Cass and Speaker stomped the snow off their boots, unwound their scarves and made for their personal stools.

"Welcome back! Elsa placed their cups in front of them. "No problems on your first drive across the ice?"

"It was easy." Speaker assured her. "The ice huts are beginning to appear already."

"The soft season is over," George mumbled.

"You sound sad," Bear, who was having his morning coffee, smiled.

"Yup, I love the soft season. You can cogitate and deliberate, in peace."

Cass leaned into his ear and whispered "And copulate!"

George smiled into his coffee.

"I wonder why we each sit on the same stool when we come here?" Speaker asked.

Clara flung open the door.

Bear stood up before even receiving whatever news she had to bring.

He settled his hat on his head. "Whenever you appear in a rush, Clara, I know something's up."

"Jack Winston called. They've found a body!"

With the cruiser blaring Bear pulled into the harbour and jumped out. "Jack?"

Winston indicated the rumpled man beside him. "This is Billie Wilkenson."

Bear turned to him. "You found a body?"

"It was my first fishing day!"

Wilkenson was obviously very unsettled. Bear led him to a bench outside Jack's tuck shop. "Tell me what happened."

"My line grabbed on something. I tried to get the hook off but it was stuck, so I pulled it till it came to the surface." He took a stuttering breath. "I could see something dark through the hole and felt it banging against the frozen surface. I kept pulling." He dug a dirty handkerchief out of his pocket, "Wish I hadn't!"

"And?"

"It was a bloated face! The hooks were in the neck and the line was wrapped around it. The eyes were protruding," he cried. "So I let the line go."

"You let it go?" Bear tried to keep his voice calm.

"I cut the line and tied it to a hook. It's still attached."

To make sure he avoided any areas where underground streams kept the ice soft, George accompanied Bear in his cruiser. An ambulance followed them and behind it a car with a diver.

"This is a lot of traffic for December ice. Hope to hell it holds." George worried. The view in his side mirror made him look over his shoulder. Cars were coming from all different directions. Black ants on the white ice. "How the hell did the news get out so fast."

"Mira!" Bear groaned.

"But you don't have a party line."

"But Jack Winston does." Bear stared at the swarm through his rear-view mirror. "We'll have to rope off the area to keep them all back."

"I can do that for you."

"Thanks, George, You'll have to do it fast. Curiosity is arriving faster than a scalded cheetah."

After setting up the perimeter, George joined Bear, Billie Wilkerson and the diver who were gathered at the door of the hut. They were all disguising emotion with falsely professional voices. Wilkerson's nose and lips danced, Bear pawed the ground with his extra-large boot and talked without looking up, and inside his mitts George cracked his knuckles.

Already clad in his dry suit, the diver took over. "Let's see what we have here." He opened the door of the hut and with quick toss of his head beckoned Bear to follow.

The single window was darkened by a cloud leaving the inside colder than the exterior and the light so poor that they had to find the line at the hole where the clear water made things brighter and follow it to the hook.

The diver took a gentle tug, "Don't want to pull any harder. It might release the hook and then I'd have a hell of a time finding the source."

"Source," seemed to Bear a strange word under the circumstances, and he said so in a whisper, not really planning to share his thought.

"What's dead is dead. If it's not a body, it's equally dead no matter what you call it!" He picked up Billie's shovel. "There are a couple more in my car. "We'll have to move the snow banking the walls and then move the hut."

The audience watched, silent, as they shoveled away the snow. The diver then stood up and looked his companions over with a critical eye. "You're the smallest, Billie, get inside and disconnect the line. Then lie flat while we lift the hut over you.

They were able to lift the makeshift hut without much difficulty and settled it down a distance from the hole. The diver then went to his car and brought out an electric saw. "The hole needs to be bigger."

As he worked, surprisingly few questions from behind the ropes were posed to Bear.

"Is it a body, Bear?"

"Don't know yet."

"If it is, do you have any idea who it might be?

"Nope," Bear lied.

The diver pulled on his dry suit hood and mitts and slipped into the hole leaving an expectant silence hovering.

It didn't take long before a body was pushed to the surface and the diver's head appeared beside it. He removed his mouth piece and hollered, "Pull it up!"

On their knees, George and Bear pulled the bloated balloon to the surface. Bear swallowed back vomit, and mouthed, "Jumper!" to George.

George nodded and shuffled close to Bear so that they could hide the body until the stretcher came to take him away.

As they watched the ambulance drive off, the diver said, "I'm going back down. I saw something else strange down there.

A few minutes later he returned and pushed a camera on to the ice before he climbed out.

Of course, Bear thought.

"His skull was bashed in but it could have happened from whatever accident caused him to drown," The chief reported over the phone.

"Do you believe that?"

"Not really, but I'm not going to put the provincials into investigating the death of that poisonous little twerp. I'll leave that up to you, Bear, and if you want to call it a drowning I'll go along with it."

Bear hung up and threw himself back in his chair. George had found so many disturbing photos in Jumper's apartment that almost anyone in town would want to bash his head in.

There was one from way back of Speaker admiring the flames of the fire he'd started. Attached to it was a newspaper article with the same picture and a report that the photo had helped convict him.

There were copies of old photos of all the men in the Captain's platoon who didn't make it home.

One of the door of the Little Brown Jug with the blind down and a closed sign. Elsa was holding it a bit open and Bear was squeezing in. And another of him with his arm over Tess's shoulder steering her out of his boathouse.

And there were many, many, more. George selling hooch from the Wawanesa, the mayor going into the whorehouse in Orville, the town doctor in a bar with his nurse, and of course, the Chief with his speared pickerel!!

His biggest worry was the pictures of the little girls which he had already destroyed after showing them to Mrs. Fraser. Had he sent those on?

What was the lethal little man planning to do with his horde? Did he want to ruin people just as he'd been ruined? Did he have an overbearing need to be powerful? Can a man be just plain evil?

Bear could imagine him holed up in his darkroom gloating over the photos, and feeling the excitement and danger of the power he was always chasing.

Everybody would be pleased if he attributed Jumper's death to drowning and forgot about it. Should he? Was he willing to tuck denial into his own mental darkroom? What kind of a cop was he?

He made a pile of the photos and sat staring at them. File them or burn them which was it to be?

"There's a whole lot of spite in that pile." Bear had been unaware George was watching him from the door.

Bear lifted the stack and balanced it in his hand "Is that how you look at it?"

"He was a venomous snake who didn't receive an ounce of admiration from anywhere. His only hope was to overwhelm with his poison."

"Do you think he was murdered?"

"Probably."

"Do you think I should find out who did it?"

"Guess that's for you to decide."

"Would you?"

"You know me, Bear. I tease the rules of the world. But you're a cop. You have to decide what kind of a cop."

"You're right."

"So what are you going to do?"

The question weighed. Minutes passed.

"I don't know, George. I really don't know."

Chapter 27

With the winter ice firmly set George could drive back and forth from the island across the ice. He climbed out of the car in front of Cass's house and grabbed the package that had arrived for her at the post office. He moved it from hand to hand. Such a light object to weigh so heavily.

"It's here!" Cass took the parcel, turned away from him and sat in the living room with the package on her knee. Carefully, she slipped open the sides of the brown paper and pulled out the book, which she held out in front of her looking critically at the cover, with her large photo beneath the title: 'Lessons From The Merry Madam'. She moved it back and forth and sideways, and looked over her shoulder at George who was leaning with his back against the kitchen counter. "It's from when I was twenty-five! Pretty hot, wasn't I?"

Her hair, then, was cut short and wispy and died beyond blond to white. Her cheekbones were emphasized by a sexy smile, and the whole look was finished off with subtle green makeup surrounding dark lashes.

"Yup." George confirmed. But not his Cass. The now Cass, the Cass he loved, had long brown hair framing a naturally beautiful face.

She put the book down and returned to the package. "There are a couple of letters here, too." She pulled them out and read them. "Georgie, listen! There's a man who wants to be my agent! He says he can get me interviews on the radio and in the newspapers and maybe even a movie!" She threw the letters in the air and kicked her legs singing, "The Merry Madam is going to be famous!"

She jumped up and without acknowledging George or even thinking about him, he suspected, she went to the mirror on the wall. "I'll cut my hair, and take it back to where it was." Then turned to George.

"I'll need to leave tomorrow in time to catch the afternoon train. Can you pick me up in the morning?"

She spoke to him without thought. He could have been the local taxi driver and her voice would have sounded the same.

He pushed himself away from the counter and replied in the same tone. "I'll be here around noon."

Her promise to him was already tarnished.

At the station, he waited as she climbed the steps. On the top step, she turned around and smiled. "They're going to love me, Georgie. There's nothing like spice to get their juices flowing!" She threw him a kiss and disappeared without a backward look.

George headed to the Little Brown Jug, accepted coffee from Elsa and without giving a damn who was looking spiked it with his own hooch.

Elsa looked at him with worry. "Is everything ok George?"

"Couldn't be better, Elsa, just put The Merry Madam on the train to fame."

"Cass is gone?"

"Her book will be out in a week or so and it's already hooked the publicity seekers. She's on her way to the big time!"

"It'll pass. She'll be back."

George almost choked on his glug of coffee. "Not so sure about that. But it's ok. I've missed being creative with Speaker."

"Be careful now, George, Bear is your friend," she smiled, "And mine, and I don't want you to put him in a quandary!"

"Means we'll have to be 'specially creative," he laughed.

"George!"

"Don't worry Elsa. We'll be good."

Chapter 28

Although still dreary, March celebrated the absence of ice and with it George's arrival via the Trent canal with Wawanesa the third. He had changed very little from the previous Wawanesa. A better engine, more comfortable seats in the rear and a seat for himself behind the wheel. He was pleased with his purchase. All it needed now was memory rubbed into the planks.

Among the mail he fetched from the post office to deliver to the island was a letter from Cass, the first since she left. He waited until he reached home and took it into his mirrored room to open it.

> Dear Georgie,
>
> I'd never have imagined the publicity the book has triggered. I'm running from here to there doing interviews. And, Georgie, yesterday I was on a program with Christopher Plummer, the Shakespearean actor and Gordie Howe, the famous hockey player. Can you imagine, me, an old whore, included in such company? The best thing is they like me. I come from a world that arouses them and their curiosity, and, you know me – I intend to take advantage of it.
>
> Toronto is booming and I'm here right in the center of it all.
>
> I'm writing to tell you that my agent has set up the possibility of a movie and I'm off to Hollywood to even bigger fame!

I'm sorry, Dear Georgie, my promise to you was made without the knowledge that I was about to become famous, and you know me well enough to realize I can't resist. I know I'm letting you down, but I'm sure you understand and wish me well.

Will you and Hawker please close my house? Who knows how long I'll be gone?

I love you Georgie, but in my own way.

Cass

He folded it, put it back in the envelope and stared at himself in the mirror. The front view showed his distress in the flat, unmoving stare. The droop of his shoulders seen from the back told him he was expecting this.

He pushed himself up from the chair and turned in a slow circle catching his reflection in the various mirrors.

You had to know, George. How could you ever believe that Cass would be content on the island that offered her no stimulation?

He threw himself back in the chair. How was it that the island created two such different characters? He, who wanted only to be the friend of Wind, Tree, Water and Sun, and she who couldn't escape them fast enough?

She was like the seed of an exotic tree that was blown on to the island but didn't thrive because it was foreign to the soil, whereas he was an old maple with roots that clung to all life beneath the surface.

He looked sternly at his reflection face on. She won't be back, so accept it Georgie and get on with life!

Some weeks later George and Hawker finished boarding up Cass's house.

Hawker fought tears. "What now, for me?"

"You're still responsible for the house, Hawker, and you can live in the cabin at the back."

"Cass, she said that? She told you to tell me? She sent the money?

"She did all those things, Hawker. She didn't forget you," George lied. "But why not come to Cedartown with me today. You need to get away, and I need your help with my new idea.

When George, Hawker and Speaker arrived at the Brown Jug, Bear was having a late breakfast. George reached into the bag he was carrying and pulled out a bottle which he plunked on the counter.

"What now?" Elsa asked, her curiosity accompanied with a smile.

"Whatever it is it damn well better be legal." Bear didn't stop eating his bacon and eggs.

Did George sense an indifference in Bear's comment? And if that was true, why? Was he considering giving up? And if that was true was he planning on leaving Cedartown? If he did, it would be damned sad. Bear was a friend even though they competed for the attention of Mistress Law. He smiled to himself. It had become a game between them, each testing the other to gain her attention.

"This is Chaga, My Friends. My cousin here, and I are partners in a new business."

Elsa picked up the bottle and stared at the contents. "It looks like tea."

"It is a tea, but a very special one. It's made from the fungus on the birch tree." He took the bottle form Elsa and twirled it. "This nectar tea cures cancer, lowers high blood pressure, prevents heart disease and enhances bedroom attentions." He put it down on the counter and stared at it. "All it needs now is a name." He looked up at them all. "Any suggestions?"

"Why not just plain 'CHAGA'. What's the matter with that?" Speaker asked.

"Not good marketing, cousin. You have to have a name that draws them in. I'll put in smaller letters all the diseases it is said to cure, but I need a good name.

"Make sure you include the words 'is said to', Bear said, "You don't want to be sued.

"Are we really cousins? I've been wondering."

George put his arm around Speaker's shoulder. "All islanders are cousins one way or another."

"How about 'HAPPY TEA'?" Elsa suggested.

"A good possibility, but I wanted something a little more suggestive."

"GEORGE'S POISON." This from Bear.

"I like it," George laughed, but I'm not sure it'll work.

Hawker said. "It is not poison. It is a good thing. I make my own chaga and drink it every day." He smiled. "And look at me!"

Everyone laughed.

Bear wiped his chin with a napkin, turned on the stool and got up to leave. "You could call it 'CHANGE-UP CHAGA'" They looked at him confused. "A change-up is a slow pitch thrown to confuse the batters timing. I think it would be appropriate."

"Not bad," Elsa added. "It suits your latest venture. Your tea will confuse disease."

"Then CHANGE-UP CHAGA it will be." He put the bottle back in its bag. "I'm off to order labels." He looked at Speaker and Hawker. "Either of you want to come?"

"I'll see you at the boat. There is a lady I promised to see."

"Annette?"

"Nope. Someone else."

George shook his head.

"I will come with you," Hawker said. "I have nothing to do here. My place is the island."

A week later Speaker and George filled the hold with three boxes of chaga bottles and an equal number of hooch. They set out, as usual, at dusk and George mastered the gentle waves as they made their way to the harbour.

A few hundred yards from their destination they saw Jack Winston standing at the end of the pier waving a red flag.

"Oh, Oh!" Speaker alerted George, "The flag's out!"

George threw the engine into a gentle reverse to keep the boat from going forward with the waves. "Quick, get the hooch out!"

Speaker dragged out the three boxes and they began to throw the bottles one by one over the side. "All done," Speaker threw the empty boxes into the hold and George put the engine in forward.

They entered the harbour slowly and drove to their usual spot but took their time docking, while two provincials and Bear waited at the edge.

One of the policemen jumped into the back. "We have to check your hold. It's been reported that you're selling home-made liquor."

"Us?" George looked at them in confusion. For a moment, he caught Bear's expression. He quickly looked away and continued with a wide-eyed expression of incomprehension.

The three boxes were brought out. "What's this?"

"It's chaga," Speaker answered.

"We sell it in town," George explained.

The policeman passed it to his partner. "Open one, we'll have to taste it."

Speaker opened a bottle and handed it to him.

The cop took a sip and handed it to his partner who tried it too. He made a face. "Taste like turpentine!"

"It's medicinal," George explained in his most practical voice. "You mix it with juice for your morning dose." He winked. "And a little extra in the evening helps a man."

Curious, the cop stared at the opened bottle. "Medicinal? What does it help?"

George showed them the small lettering on the bottle that enumerated all the unfortunate ills CHANGE-UP CHAGA could prevent, and then went into suggestive details of why it was best placed on the bedside table.

By the time he was finished with his description the cops had entirely forgotten the original reason for entering the boat, and said their farewells.

George saw them off to their cruiser, each with a bottle in his hand.

Bear shook his head at the pair, but, but as he was turning away, George caught a smile sneaking out the corner of his lips

The next morning Bear walked to the end of the pier and a few hundred yards out, saw four or five boats anchored. People were diving from the boats and from time to time came up out of the water with bottles.

Chapter 29

Early morning. Bear sat in Elsa's living room and stared off into space. There were so many people who hated Jumper, almost anyone could have murdered him. Should he pursue it?

Having dressed for the day, Elsa tucked herself in beside him on the sofa. "Where are you?"

He put his arm around her and pulled her in closer "Do you think a person can be completely evil?"

"Jumper?"

"Umm-hmm. I can't figure out why he spent his life trying to hurt people."

"We'll never know. I guess evil is a disease that affects us all, we're none of us free of it, but in some it's worse than in others. In the bad cases, I believe it disturbs the mind"

Bear felt uncertain. "He seemed to enjoy causing pain. I can imagine him gloating over each successive cruelty."

"You're probably right, but did it make him a happy man?"

They remained silent, contemplating their words.

After a few minutes, Bear kissed the top of her head. "Do you think I should investigate his murder: find the killer?"

She pushed away from him, and with her hand, gently brushed his cheek. "That's what's worrying you?"

"I'm tempted to leave it alone. It's what the Captain wants. He thinks attributing Jumper's death to drowning is the most acceptable solution."

"And you?"

"I'm in a quandary about even remaining a cop." He stood up and went to stare out the window. "I'm already turning a blind eye on petty crimes. But this is murder and if I ignore it I'm condoning it." He turned to her. "Does that mean I should not be a cop?"

Elsa put her arms around his waist. "I have a selfish reason for wanting you to remain a cop, so I can't help you this time, Bear, personal interest interferes." She took her apron from the hook and opened the door to go down to her restaurant. "All I can say is that you're a good man and a good cop, and I love you." She gave him a wan smile. "There! I've said it." She went out and shut the door behind her.

"I love you too," he whispered at the closed door, which didn't help at all. He strapped on his belt, took his hat and mumbled, "And I love being a cop, too." Perhaps one decision would ease him into the other.

In the office, Clara was typing up the report of Jumper's death.

Bear sat down across from her. "Do you think he drowned?"

Without looking up Clara said, "Of course not. A man like that was inviting a good person to commit an evil act. It was his final success."

"Any ideas you might have as to who did it?"

Clara stopped typing, and leaned forward over her machine. "I could suggest ten possibilities, and give you the names of many more who are pleased he is gone."

"The Captain says to attribute the cause to drowning."

With her head, she gestured at the paper in the scroll of her typewriter. "And that's what I'm writing right now."

Bear bit his upper lip. "I think I should pursue it."

"Leave it alone, Bear," Clara said with severity. "We're rid of a vicious little man who enjoyed destroying people, An investigation would hurt too many townspeople and it would ruin the respect they have for you."

Bear got up. "This is all becoming too much. I'm going fishing!"

It was calming out on the water. He steered towards the shoal off Meek's Point. Thanks to George he now knew all the best spots. The water was flat and clear and he could see the bottom. He put his head back and took a huge sniff of the cold, pure air. The sky was without a cloud.

How could he leave?

He remembered his Dad saying to him, "If you can count your friends on the fingers of one hand, you're a damned lucky man." He smiled at the memory. Such statements usually followed the third drink, but were, nevertheless, often profound.

He looked down at his hand, and lifted the first finger: Elsa, the second, Clara, then George and Speaker and Cass. He had already started on the second hand, needing fingers for his Captain, and Mrs. Fraser and little Essie. He tossed out a line. And Tess.

Where else would he enjoy so many strange friendships? If he decided to remain a cop he would not be the kind of police officer he'd imagined himself to be when he arrived in Cedartown, after he'd been kicked out of town for exposing fraud within the ranks. He'd been so right in those days, so correct, unbending, and severe. What had softened him? Affection for the likes of George and Speaker and Cass? Love of Elsa? He reeled in a bite. Or what happened with young Tess? Had it not been for George he would have - - - it hurts him to think of it.

The fish got away.

Chapter 30

Six months of the year Mother Nature tested the durability of nature and man. May brought the promise of summer on the island; her reward for the survivors.

The bug-protecting hinge on the screened door pulled it shut in a bang when George left and went down to the lake. Even that noise was a familiar echo of summer.

From his dock, he dove in and began a three mile swim the length of the shoreline to Cass's house.

With a long slow crawl, he stretched into each stroke with the pleasure of being alive. Face-down he passed minnows rushing in and out of rocks, and twice saw a small mouthed bass making a snatch for one. When he turned his head to the right for air he felt the evergreens standing sentinel and creating quiet reflections through which he swam. On the left, Sky blanketed the water and him.

He climbed up the rocks at Cass's shore and went in search of Hawker. The dogs found him first but changed their barks to tail-wagging squeals when they recognized George.

Hawker appeared from the back of his cabin with a red-tailed hawk on his arm.

"Damn-me!" George exclaimed, "That's why you're called Hawker. I never knew."

Wrinkled-up eyes and a huge smile appeared on his innocent face, but, George was sure the huge half-breed with a large hawk on his arm would scare the b'Jesus out of anyone who didn't know him.

"The name it came from when I was a kid and had a hawk. The hawk, it did not last. The name it stuck."

"What are you doing with it, now?"

"The bird, it was injured when I found it. I made it better. Now I am trying to teach it to work with the dogs."

"Explain that to me."

"The bird, it catches the squirrel and the rabbit but it does not want to bring it home. If it will let the dog have it the dog will bring it home."

"How's it going?"

"The bird, it is like Cass. It wants its own treat."

"Right." George sat down on a large boulder, and Hawker sat down beside him, unaware that the bird was too close for George's liking. He moved as far over as the boulder would allow. "Can't you put the damned thing away while we talk?"

Hawker looked at the bird as though he was ignorant of its presence, but took it to its home somewhere behind his cabin.

He returned and sat beside George. "Cass, when will she be back?"

"I guess when her fame dies down."

"That could be a long time."

"Could be. Might be. Probably will be," George decided. "Do you mind staying?"

"Cass was good to me. I will look after her place."

"Come over to the harbour and I'll give you the money Cass sent.

He went back into the water and began the long pleasant crawl along the shore of the island. His Home.

Back from the trip across the lake in the Wawanesa, Speaker was waiting for him on his dock with a letter in his hand. "It's from Cass." He handed George his towel and George dried off well before accepting the letter. "Let's go up to the porch and make ourselves comfortable before we open it."

With beers on the table between them George sat back in his chair and stared at the envelope. "It's only the second note in a year." He looked over at Speaker. "What do you think, good news or bad?"

"I figure if she hasn't written she doesn't need our help so it must be good."

"Let's see." He opened the envelope, read it twice and then handed it over to Speaker and took a swig of beer.

Speaker read it aloud.

Dear Georgie,

This is the life! When I'm the center of attention, Georgie, I am more of everything: more beautiful, more intriguing, and even more talented! My voice and conversation pulls them in like hooked bass, and I love the admiration! It's honey for my innards! I'll do anything to keep it going for as long as possible.

They're offering me a lot of money to write a second book, but this time, a real exposé. I'll probably do it. You know me, Georgie. I need that syrup in my breast!

I don't think I'll need the house any more. Could you put it on the market for me? You have my power of attorney so you can do the whole thing yourself. I'm sorry. I love you Georgie, but I'm afraid I love this life more.

Kiss everyone for me, and keep an eye out in the newspapers for the latest escapade in the life of The Merry Madam!

I send kisses to Speaker and all your friends and devoted love to you.

Speaker handed back the letter and took some beer himself. "How do you feel?"

"Don't know," George answered, and he didn't. Can he have a broken heart and still be relieved?

Chapter 31

Clara interrupted Bear's confused reveries. Sniffing back tears, she handed him the Globe and Mail.

THE MERRY MADAM, MURDERED.

Cassandra, Toronto's famous "Merry Madam" was shot to death last night in a hotel in Hollywood where she was participating in the making of a film about her career, the history of a woman who spent her life granting sexual pleasures to anyone who was willing to pay her exorbitant fee.

He skipped the voyeuristic paragraphs about her life as a prostitute and then a Madam with her own group of girls, and went down to the end of the article.

Police say that signs point to a professional murder, and suggest that it could have been because Cassandra was in the process of writing a 'grand exposé' about the important men she had serviced.

Her ashes will be transported to Toronto and buried in the home of her birth.

"You'll have to get to George before anyone else."

"The Wawanesa has already gone back. I'll take my boat."

Clara pulled out a handkerchief and rubbed her eyes. "It's better that way. You can tell him when he's in his own home." She smiled a sad smile. "I knew her as a kid, wandering around town with George in tow. I was never sure if she was dragging him along or if he was watching over her." She inhaled a huge sob. "In the last year, being her friend has been an adventure I would never have believed myself to be involved in!"

Bear trudged up the path to George's house, half-hoping he wouldn't be home.

He knocked on the screen door and went in calling his name. George squeezed out of a small room off the kitchen. He quickly closed it behind him, but not before Bear caught sight of a sliver of mirror shining through the small opening. His curiosity was piqued but it wasn't the moment. Bear grimaced and looked away from his friend.

"Bear?" George's tone was loaded with preparation for the unexpected.

Unable to say the words he handed George the newspaper.

Bear wasn't sure how many times George read it through before lifting his head and staring out at the lake.

"I have to be alone, Bear."

"You sure?"

George didn't answer. He went into the room with the mirror and closed the door.

Bear sighed, unsure what to do but felt he had to do something. He went down to the harbour and found Speaker loading the Wawanesa with furniture, while an elderly couple looked on. "It's sad, but we're too old for the island," The old woman smiled around her wrinkles. "It hurts to go,' the hunched man added, "but I guess every man has to accept when his body can't behave enough to do for himself."

Bear smiled absently, and climbed down into the boat to speak to Speaker, who was loading the life of the couple into the hold. "Bad news," he said quietly.

Speaker stood up. "What? Who?"

"Cass has been murdered."

Speaker fell back against the side of the boat and slid down along the wall. He angrily wiped a tear that was moistening his eye, and shook his head over and over. "No reins could keep that dame harnessed, not even George." He wiped his running nose. "How?"

"In Hollywood. Police think it was professional. I guess she'd tempted the public with the idea of a tell-all book, and there were some who didn't want it to happen." He sat down beside him and picked up a leaf that had been trampled on the bottom of the boat, threw it in the water and watched it float away half submerged by the waves that licked it. "George said he needed to be alone. Shut himself up in that room off the kitchen.

"That's good."

"Good?"

"It's his place. It's where he figures things out." Speaker pushed his long hair away from his face. "Don't worry, Bear."

George stood in the middle of the room. His body felt wrapped in a cold blanket that held his reaction tight within him. He stared at himself, unblinking, wishing he could remain cold and without thought and unexposed to a reaction forever. But he became hot, and anger seeped through his pours and the blanket fell aside. Damn you, Cass. You couldn't stay away from danger and attention. You left me.

He grabbed the newspaper, and tore, it and tore it until it was in shreds and then stomped on it. And he stopped and stared up at himself and smiled in embarrassment. You got everything you asked for, even fame at the end, and damn you, Cass, you left me stamping like an angry little boy.

He threw himself in the chair, waved his hand at her ghost and his own image. Goodbye, you tough beautiful broad. I loved you.

And he cried.

Chapter 32

George slouched in the back of the Wawanesa waiting for Speaker to arrive with the mail and any passengers who wanted to go to the island.

It had been two weeks since Cass's death and the world was still a blur. His limbs were heavy and the electricity of life had dimmed. He knew it would pass, but he wished to hell the passing would quicken up.

Speaker brought their truck to a screeching halt, jumped out and banged the door so hard George winced. Every movement Speaker made was heavy-handed and hurried. It usually made George smile.

"Here's the mail, partner. There's one for you."

George stared at the envelope Speaker handed him. The top left corner said 'McLaren, Stern & Johnston, Attorneys at Law.'

Not wanting to know the words he expected, he opened it slowly and plodded through it. "It's from Cass's lawyer." he said in a flat voice without looking up. "He wants to come out and read us her will. "It says, Walter Bear McKinley and a man named Hawker should be present."

"And not me?"

"Don't let it upset you. The only thing a will does is weigh you down with responsibility," he mumbled, "and that's something neither of us wants."

"I guess you're right, but it hurts just the same."

"It says he needs to know Hawker's full name. You know what it is?"

"Nope, he's always been just 'Hawker'. We've had no need to harness him with anything more." He sat on the bench beside George. "But why Hawker and not me?"

"We'll see soon enough.'

Two weeks later, the three sat on Bear's deck staring out at the harbour, each tangled in his own thoughts

Bear looked at his watch. "He's late."

"Probably hit traffic."

"Should have thought of that."

"Got proof of your full name Hawker?" George asked.

Hawker pulled out a certificate of birth from the Catholic Church, and handed it to George. "I did not have anything. The priest, he found this."

"Benoit Prevert! Prevert! There's a plot of land on the north end of the island called Prevert Point. Are you that Prevert?"

"Oui. There was a cabin there. It was my only home. My father, he was Jacques Prevert, a fur trader like me. My mother she was Chippewa from the reservation on the on the big island to the south. I stayed in that cabin with my mother until I was old enough to trap with my father. Each year we came back to the cabin, but when my father drowned, I took over his trap lines and my mother went back to her island; she said her roots had wound themselves around her heart."

"I remember the old cabin on Prevert Point when I was a kid, but it's not there now. It burned down, didn't it?"

"Oui, I believe some kids from the mainland found it empty and used it for their pleasures."

"What did you do then? Where did you go?"

"It was the year I lost my toes. The story, it appeared in the Cedartown Express."

"I would think so," Bear joined into the conversation. "It was a mind-teasing story. You cut off your own toes to keep from freezing to death. It would fill the readers with wonder about you and about themselves."

"Cass, she read the article and found me in the Toronto Hospital. I have worked for her every day since then."

"But you must still own the land on Prevert Point." George insisted.

Hawker shook his head. "The cabin it burned I have no papers. Perhaps my father, he settled there without asking."

"It could be," Bear agreed, "But we'll check with the town clerk to be sure."

"I hear a car," George looked at Bear and knew that he, too, was worried about the hidden papers Cass had given him. George prayed they were well hidden.

He had an open collar with a gold chain around his neck. His finger nails were manicured. They sat around Bear's only table and the threesome waited while the lawyer removed papers from his briefcase.

"Cass was a friend of all of us at McLaren's. She was our client throughout her whole career." He smirked at them suggestively. "We 'took care of things' for her." He shuffled his papers. "We're sorry about her death." He said without emotion.

"We were her friends!" Hawker corrected him.

George smiled. Good for you, Hawker.

"Of course you were." The lawyer didn't look up. "Let's get on with it." And he preceded with the preamble "I, Cassandra Warren being of sound mind bequeath to Hawker Prevert the cabin on my property and a half acre surrounding it and $1,000.00 in recognition of all our years together. The rest of my estate including my house on the island and $100,000.00, goes to my dearest friend George Brown"

Upset, George turned off the man's droning and seethed with anger. Until he rid himself of Cass's fuck money his breathing space would be in tangles.

The lawyer pulled out another paper. "Before she left for Hollywood Cass added a codicil in which she left her car and her boat to Walter 'Bear' McKinley, and this box." He handed Bear a small jewelry box. "To the village she left all the cash earned from her book."

A tease even in death aren't you My Cass? Cedartown will love being the recipient of monies_made from The Merry Madam!

He watched Bear open the jewelry box. Inside was a diamond ring and a note, which elicited a tight-lipped smile.

"What does it say?"

"To be used when you're ready." Bear read aloud.

The lawyer handed a check to Hawker and said to George, "You'll have to come to the office to arrange for the transfer of funds and ownership of the house. You want to make a date now?"

George did not want to go to the city. He did not want $100,00.00 or Cass's house, but it would be pretty damned difficult to say no. He agreed to an appointment later in the month.

"Finally," the lawyer asked, George, "Did Cassandra leave any papers with you?"

Feigning innocence, "Papers?" George asked. "What kind of papers?"

"Cassandra threatened to expose a lot of people in her next book. She must have made notes and kept them somewhere.

"Not with me," George insisted.

"You sure?" The lawyer looked at him with disbelief.

"No, she gave me nothing. She didn't even talk about it."

"Except when the head of the Toronto Police Force arrived on the island."

"Nope, not even then. I think that came up when she was in Hollywood teasing anyone who would listen."

"She must have made some notes."

"If she did I don't know about it."

The lawyer shoved his papers into his briefcase. "If you do have anything, you'd better burn it. Your life could depend on it."

They listened to him descend the stairs. Hawker looked at his check. "Cass was my real friend. I will go back to the island now, and think."

As soon as he was gone George whispered to Bear, as though the lawyer was still there. "You still have all those papers?

"Behind a panel under the life preservers."

"What're you going to do with them."

"Get rid of them fast. I'll send them to a reporter on the Globe and Mail and let them deal with it."

"Do it today." He rubbed Bear's sleeve. I'm going for a walk on the pier to think.

"You're not happy with your inheritance?"

"It's a weight."

Speaker was waiting outside. As they walked to the end of the pier, George explained the content of Cass's will.

"She could have left me something. A remembrance of some kind."

George put his arm over Speaker's shoulder. "Yes, she should have, cousin. But it's better that she didn't. Any little thing left to you would be a continual reminder of Cass, and we need to forget her."

"We do? Why?"

"Not sure I can explain it. There's a heaviness that comes with love. It climbs into the body and tightens life with worry and responsibility, and we don't want that, do we?"

"I guess not." Speaker answered with a frown.

Without any more words they walked together to the end of the pier. Sun warmed the wind that was making whitecaps on the lake. George had to face it. Cass's death had been a release. He was no longer chained to a preposterous devotion. But Cass was not going to let him go. Now he was strapped with her money and her home, and he didn't want either.

They arrived at the end of the pier, leaned on the wall overlooking the lake and watched the waves bash up against the cement.

"What are you going to do?"

"I'll have to give it all away." He put his hand on Speaker's shoulder and smiled. "The question is, how? We'll have to think on it. They sauntered back to Bear's house creating and disposing of ideas.

There was a red Cadillac with white wall tires in front of Bear's boathouse.

"That's not from around here." George frowned. "I don't like it."

They picked up their pace but, before reaching Bear's boathouse, the sound of a gunshot pierced the air.

Both men ran towards the door which was off the latch. Speaker, the faster of the two, tore it open and was almost knocked over by a man with a gun in his right hand and a large brown envelope in the left. Face to face with Speaker, he lifted the gun to shoot again, but George charged him from the side and the shot missed Speaker who kicked out at the weapon hand, dislodging it, and then went for the man's jaw with his head. The culprit fell unconscious.

"Watch him," George demanded and rushed into the boathouse. Bear was sitting on the floor holding his leg which was gushing blood.

"I think he got the artery." Bear winced in pain.

"Lie down!" George ordered, and lifted his leg until it was higher than his heart. He pulled a bench under the leg and grabbed a beach towel and applied pressure. Bear was looking woozy, he wouldn't be able to keep up the pressure, With one hand, he removed his belt and made a tourniquet. "I'll get to a phone for an ambulance."

He grabbed some rope from a hook and threw it out to Speaker then tore up the stairs to Bear's apartment where he turned the telephone knob harder than necessary. When she answered, he yelled, "Mira, call an ambulance, and the Provincials! Bear's been shot at his boathouse." Then ran back down the stairs.

Speaker called from outside. "What's happening?"

"Keep an eye out for the ambulance!" George wasn't sure how long he was supposed to leave the tourniquet. Frightened of causing more damage, he released it and applied as much pressure as he could to the artery. Blood spurted around his hand. He tightened the tourniquet again. "I hope to Hell they get here fast!"

Although he knew it had only been a few minutes, it felt to George that he'd been attending to Bear for hours before the ambulance came. He followed the stretcher out the door. Speaker stood over the attacker who was tied up and sitting against the wall of the boathouse. His head was collapsed on his chest. George didn't have time to ask what Speaker had done. "I'll go with Bear. You wait for the Provincials."

"What do you want me to do with this?" Speaker held up the brown envelope.

"I'll take it."

In the ambulance Bear was given morphine. His eyes began to droop but before falling off he mumbled. "Get rid of that envelope, Fast!" His head lolled to the side, "I need Elsa," and he was out.

At the hospital Bear was rushed into the emergency room. The swing doors closed behind the stretcher leaving George stranded. He went in search of a phone and dialed the Cedartown exchange. When Mira answered, he said "Put me through to Elsa, Mira."

"She's on her way to the hospital." The familiar voice answered. "How is Bear?"

"He'll manage. Have you talked to Clara?"

"She's on her way, too."

"What do you know about Speaker?"

"Sorry, no messages from him, but I heard the Provincials are on their way."

"You heard."

"The lines have been very busy with the news."

He shook his head, hung up, and found a plastic chair in the cold uninviting room, where he sat, helpless, worried, waiting, wondering, planning. The adrenaline flowing through him was acute. Bear had seeped into the realm of true friendship. So involved with his preoccupations, he jumped when Elsa touched his shoulder.

She was shaking "Is Bear?"

He stood up and embraced her trembling body. "He was shot in the leg. They're fixing him up right now. He'll be ok."

She collapsed in the chair. "All Mira said was that he'd been shot." Tears rolled down her cheeks. "I was imagining the worst."

He put his arm around her and pulled her towards him. Her head collapsed on his shoulder. They were in the same position when Clara rushed in.

"What happened? Is Bear alright?"

George stood and picked up the brown envelope. He put his arm over Clara's shoulder, and steered her away from Elsa. "Cass is back to haunt us. She wrote down the names of all the city elites who had been serviced by her and her girls and included information on fraud and other criminal undertakings." He tapped the envelope on his knee. Should he burden Clara with the responsibility?

"That's what you have in that envelope?"

"Cass gave it to Bear when the city closed down her house, to be publicized in case she was murdered."

Clara grimaced in anger. "She suspected even then! Why in God's name did she announce to the world that she was going to write an exposé?"

"I know, Clara, I know. But the last thing I want to do right now is rehash Cass's vanity."

"What happened with Bear?"

"When Cass's lawyer came to see us about her will he wanted to know what we knew. I guess he didn't believe us when we said we had no information, so he sent a thug to make sure. We'll have to wait for Bear to tell us what happened." He put the envelope in Clara's hand. "Bear will be ok but neither of us is safe until this has been published." His throat hurt with all the anxious talking. "Bear said you knew someone important at the paper."

"I do. She's the daughter of a friend. Has her own byline. I'll phone her from here and either drive to the city or, if she can, meet her half way."

"When the news is spread it should neutralize the danger." George hoped. "Be extra careful Clara."

On her way out, Clara stopped and kissed Elsa. "I have to do something for Bear. I'll come back as soon as possible."

"Are you going back to Cedartown? I left the restaurant in a rush."

"No, I'm not but I wouldn't worry. Mira will call in help."

Elsa gave a wry smile. "Something to be said for our backward town."

Once Bear was settled in his room, groggy but conscious, his first words to George were, "The envelope?"

"Taken care of," George assured him.

"The doctor said you probably saved his life by applying the tourniquet," Elsa looked up from massaging Bear's hand.

"Damn! Bear mumbled. "Not a man to be in debt to!" He smiled. "Thanks, my friend."

George laughed. "Now you owe me. A dangerous thing for a cop."

"Could be a lame cop," Bear moaned.

"We'll keep you anyway, won't we Elsa?"

She kissed Bear's hand and nodded.

George left the two lovebirds and borrowed Elsa's car to drive back to Cedartown.

Jack Winston was waiting at the harbour. "Speaker had to go with the provincials to make a report. He said he'd meet you back here, but there are a lot of passengers in the Wawanesa expecting to be taken to the island."

"I'll take them over, get a change of clothes and come back for Speaker. Tell him to wait as I'll have to return Elsa's car to the hospital and he'll have to follow."

At the island, he went quickly to change his shirt. Half way along the path, he stopped. The screen door was weaving on its hinges and the mosquito netting was torn. He foresaw the destruction of the interior before getting up the front steps, and he was not wrong. Torn cushions, feathers flying, slashed mattress, spilled flour and salt, art torn off the wall and smashed. Complete chaos. Believing he had the papers the shooter had come here before attacking Bear. And his mirrored room? He hesitated before opening the door. The mirrors still stood: silent sentinels, but the one he faced and the one at his back each had a jagged crack. He picked up his chair that had been knocked over and stared. The cracks would stay. He didn't like them. They interfered, but that was life.

Back at Cedartown, Speaker was waiting and as George threw the ropes out to him, called, "How did it go with the provincials?

"No problem for me, but I think they have their hands full with that son of a bitch. Seems he's connected to the big brass in the city."

"That may change soon," George mumbled.

"Did you get those papers you told me about to the press?"

"Clara is doing that right now." He climbed out of the Wawanesa. "We'd better get Elsa's car back."

At the hospital, Bear was asleep.

"They want to keep him for a while to make sure there are no blood clots," Elsa whispered.

"Anything we can do?" George asked.

"We could help at the Brown Jug," Speaker offered.

Elsa looked hesitant "Well, I'm not leaving here, and poor Alice, who has been helping me since her little boy died, is alone. If you wouldn't mind maybe you and Speaker could give her a hand."

"Of course we can!" Speaker jumped in with a smile.

"But no nonsense, please!"

"Us?" Speaker asked innocently. "What kind of nonsense could we get up to? We just want to help."

"There'll be no nonsense," George assured her. "I'll leave Speaker to help Alice while I do the Wawanesa runs, otherwise, it will be Speaker, Alice and myself."

"Thank you." Elsa's smile was hesitant.

When they arrived at The Little Brown Jug, they found Alice holding things together but looking exhausted. Speaker went behind the counter, put his arm around her waist and steered her to a stool. "Relax, it's my turn now."

"Will you two be alright? I have to take a run with the Wawanesa and I'll be a while." He hadn't mentioned the chaos he'd found in his house but thought he might try to get a start at the mess. "I could be a few hours."

"Don't worry about us." Speaker assured him. "What could go wrong?"

George didn't want to think about it.

Three ten-year-old boys knelt on their stools and asked for hamburgers.

"Good thing you asked boys, because I can make you the best hamburger ever put together in this town, maybe even in the whole country!"

He dug the minced beef out of the fridge and onions and garlic and ketchup and mustard and peppers. He chopped the vegetables and threw them in a bowl with the minced beef, then added glugs of ketchup and mustard. With both hands, he dug into the jumble and began to mix with his hands.

"You should wash your hands, "Alice whispered.

Speaker looked at his coated hands, and winked at Alice. "Adds to the taste." He started to make patties but they kept falling apart.

"You need eggs to hold them together." Alice instructed.

With hands covered in the mush Speaker opened the fridge, pushed things aside until he found the eggs. He broke one into the mixture.

Alice, gripping her head with both hands and not even daring to look up moaned, "The eggs need to be beaten."

The search for a bowl for the eggs involved opening cupboards which left ketchup-laced, minced beef hand prints wherever he searched. Once he'd cracked the eggs into the bowl he needed a utensil to beat them, involving a further search through numerous drawers. Once the beaten eggs were added, the hamburgers held their shape. "That works," he laughed. "Now for the world's best hamburgers!" He threw them on the grill.

When George arrived, Alice's head was collapsed on folded arms, the adult clients were staring wide-eyed and the three kids had ketchup around their mouths as they ate oversized hamburgers.

The whole area behind the counter, wall, fridge front, drawers and counters were splattered with a two-dimensional mass of meat and ketchup.

George hit his forehead in exasperation.

Speaker was rubbing his hands on his technicolor apron as he looked at him. "What?"

Chapter 33

A week later, an exhausted George visited Bear in the hospital while Elsa went home to rescue the LBJ from Speaker. At least they had cleaned up the disaster of the first day, and damn it, Speaker's hamburgers had become the number one order.

Bear was on crutches hobbling along the hallway.

"Looking better," George comforted him.

"I'd be better out of here," He grumbled. "The air stinks of illness, the noise of pain, and the respirator sounds like death! It's not a good place to be, George."

"When will you be discharged?"

"They say a few days more, damn it." He limped back to his room and collapsed in the chair.

"Do something for me, will you, George?"

"Anything."

"That box with the ring is in the drawer beside my bed. Will you bring it to me?"

George smiled. "You're going to do it?"

"The only good thing that's come from that bullet is the realization that I want Elsa forever."

"Best decision you've ever made." George grabbed him on the shoulder and shook his hand. "It also has to mean you're staying in Cedartown,"

"That was the hardest part. It's a weight, but worth it."

"And you'll stay a cop?"

"Yes, a very lame one."

"I'll get the ring right away before you change your mind." George started to leave. "You've warmed the cockles of my heart, my man!"

"Before you go. With all this, we haven't discussed your inheritance, and what you plan to do about it."

"Don't know yet." George answered from the door. "Get rid of it somehow."

With Elsa at his side, Bear hobbled along the hall on his crutches. They were forced to come to a rapid stop as nurses and doctors tore into the hospital room in front of them. As they passed the room they could see a doctor bent over the patient applying artificial respiration as another was detaching paddles from a machine. He shook his head. "Can I convince you to help me check out of this place?"

"You really have to stay until the doctors decide. They know best, Bear." She put her arm through his, and kissed him on the cheek. "You never struck me as being so impatient."

"I don't like being in a place where I sniff illness and death all day long." They continued along the hall in silence.

In his room, she helped him into his bed.

"What if I gave you a bribe?" He smiled. "Would you help me check out then?"

"Not even then!" She said with determination as she lifted his legs on to the bed. "If you went home now, there would be nobody to help you and I can't imagine you navigating the boathouse stairs on your own."

"But if I knew of someone who might be willing to take care of me, would you help me then?"

"No, Bear. Be patient, it won't be much longer. Anyway, who could you get?"

He pulled her to him, kissed her and reached under his pillow to retrieve the box with the ring. "You," he said gently. "Will you marry me, Elsa?"

Tears flooded her eyes. "You'll stay in Cedartown?"

"I will." There, he'd done it.

She let him put Cass's ring on her finger, flung her arms around him and answered in a throaty voice. "Pack-up!"

He laughed and they kissed long and hard before he threw his legs over the bed and prepared to dress.

Until he was on his feet Bear stayed in Elsa's apartment so that she could work and have him near. They were both in the restaurant when George and Speaker arrived with The Globe and Mail.

Without a word, George unfolded it in front of Bear, leaned beside him, and pointed to the headlines.

Sensing their silence as they read, Elsa came around the counter and leaned on Bear's shoulder as she read it aloud.

FRAUD IN CITY HALL
Construction and Real Estate payoffs.
THE MERRY MADAM'S FINAL GESTURE.

A lot of corrupt deals were apparently decided in her red-draped living room, and the recently murdered Madam Cassandra had taken note of it all, which she had ordered revealed in case of her death. The papers provided enough information to give law-enforcement proofs of bribes paid by Edison Construction to win the contract for construction of the subway, and to enable Case Reality to purchase a prime package of lakeshore property that was owned by the city.

To the embarrassment of many of the city's elite, Cassandra also included the names of her patrons and their sexual preferences. As she did not include proof of their visits, The Globe has decided not to publish the names.

When she was finished, George massaged his ear and looked off into space.

Bear put his arm around his shoulder. "It's done."

"She really wasn't an island person," Speaker intoned, "But she was one hell of a dame."

"That she was," George agreed, with a frog in his throat.

Chapter 34

"You two looked dressed for a christening!" Jack Winston teased as Speaker and George, looking especially clean and respectable, tied up the Wawanesa.

"Have to go to the city," George explained.

"Not an appealing task," Jack commiserated, as the pair headed towards the truck.

Speaker kicked the rusted door of the truck to encourage it to open. "You could at least spend some of the money on a new truck, partner. This babe might drop her engine any day."

"You're right. We might stop at the Ford place on the way back."

"You mean you'll spend some of Cass's money on us?"

"Nope. We'll buy the truck on time." It would smudge his feelings for Cass if he spent any of her money. How did Cass save one hundred thousand dollars, anyway? It hurt to think of the possibilities.

Once on the highway, Speaker, having realized, by the set of George's mouth that he was not to receive any more explanation, changed the subject. "Are you worried about this lawyer-guy? Is that why you asked me to come with you?"

"You're my best company partner."

Once they hit the outskirts of the city the traffic was bumper to bumper, initiating a controlled silence inside the truck. Not at all sure where he was going, George was forced to cut in front of a Mercedes to make a left, causing an angered reaction. "Get the hell back to the country where you belong, hayseeds!"

Before he could stop him, Speaker was out of the truck and standing in front of the Mercedes. "Your balls are big when you yell from behind the wheel. Get out of your car and say that again to my face." He kicked the front fender, and headed to the driver's door where he grabbed the handle, and, in anger, tried to open it. "C'mon, yellow belly, get out of there and repeat your words," He yelled.

Swallowing hard, and staring straight ahead, the driver pressed the accelerator and whipped past the furor.

Back in the car George reacted with silence.

"What?" Speaker demanded.

"You're going to have to control that temper, cousin, especially at the lawyer's office."

"That idiot deserved it. I can control my temper when I want to."

"You've been known to lose it."

"When?"

George looked over at him, "How about when the ministers of the churches were pontificating about Frenchie's sin?"

"I would have liked to bash their heads in, you're right about that, but I didn't, did I? I just yelled a bit too much."

"And when Jumper showed Malcolm the photographs of the soldiers he'd left behind?"

"I could have strangled the little twerp, but I didn't."

They were quiet. George wondering how he was going to phrase the next question and Speaker staring out the window looking insulted.

The silence dragged until, George finally asked. "Did you kill Jumper, Speaker."

His, cousin, friend, and partner, shook his head. "I was tempted more than once, but Alice calmed me down."

"Alice?" George asked with surprise.

"Um-hmm. We've been close since we took care of The Brown Jug for Elsa while Bear was in the hospital.

"Close? How close?"

Speaker smiled a gentle smile but didn't answer.

"She has a husband, cousin."

"I know, but poor thing, with a husband in prison and a child gone, she needs a little attention."

"Go carefully partner. She is fine china."

"I know that, George. But a person can't live without feeling a touch;

a hand on the arm, a hug around the shoulders or a kiss on the cheek. It was the worst part of prison, and I won't let her suffer like that."

There was no answer to that. Speaker continued to surprise him.

"What time's your appointment?"

George could feel his tension as they sat, unmoving in the honking traffic.

"Eleven o'clock."

"I don't think you'll make it."

"I'm in no hurry to receive money I don't want."

"But I'm in a hurry to get back home where I can feel the wind tickle my skin. Anyway, there are things you could do with the money, cousin."

"I'm not spending any of Cass's money on us!"

"Not even a little? Cass meant it for you."

"Not one damned cent!"

"You are one stubborn S.O.B. cousin." Speaker smiled to soften his words. "What are you going to do with it?"

"I'm thinking on it."

"If you need any help, I'm here."

Finally, they pulled up in front of a flat-faced red brick building, which boasted its lack of ostentation with a heavy black lacquered door adorned with rubbed bronze knocker and handle. A small black sign over the knocker said, in the same gold: McLaren, Stein & Johnston, and on the next line—Attorneys at Law. It gave the impression of a very upright, old and dignified firm. They were not deceived.

At the reception, George rumbled, "I'm George Brown. I have an 11.00 o'clock appointment with Mr. Johnston.

The receptionist looked at them with interest. Gnawing on a big hunk of chewing gum, she stood from behind her desk and rested her arms on the counter that separated them, and asked with a gum-limiting smile, "You two from out of town?"

Speaker leaned away from the counter close to her. "How can you tell? Do we look different?"

She smiled, and answered in a husky voice, "Beautiful men in country clothes on beautiful bodies!"

"Mr. Johnston's office? Our 11.00 o'clock appointment." George interrupted.

"Second floor, elevator on your right," she answered without taking her eyes off Speaker.

George and Speaker turned to the elevator.

"Will you be around this evening?" She called after them.

"Looked like she was chewing her cud," Speaker whispered.

They were made to wait before being showed in to the gold-chained lawyer who did not get up to greet them or even lift his eyes from the document on the desk. "You lied when you said you didn't have Cassandra's notes."

"And you obviously didn't believe me so you sent thugs to find them," George growled. "Who tried to kill my friend, and almost succeeded."

"Wasn't me." He shifted the uppermost paper to the side and looked up at them with a sarcastic smile.

"Of course it wouldn't have been him, cousin," Speaker interrupted. He then leaned over the desk into the lawyer's face. "Don't be so God damned cocky. I met your kind in prison; there because someone gave them away." Speaker grabbed a pencil from the lawyer's holder and broke it in half. "Could be the man we caught will be the one to get you."

George squeezed Speaker's arm. "Enough, cousin. Let's get this done and get out of here."

Speaker threw himself in a chair and glared.

The lawyer, failing in his attempt to appear tough slid three documents across the desk at George so aggressively they would have fallen to the floor had George not stopped them en route. "Sign these and I'll give you the check and we're done!" His anger could not hide the fear mixed in the tone.

City traffic stayed conversation until they reached the highway.

Speaker asked, "Any thought yet on what to do with the money? You said you were thinking on it."

George took time to answer. "You remember all the kids Clara and Andrew fostered?"

"I remember. What's that got to do with the money?"

"Clara told me that many foster homes were in existence only for the money the owners received from the government to pay for the care of the kids and that often those poor kids were badly treated."

"You're not thinking of taking in foster kids, are you? You wouldn't know what to do with them!"

"Of course I'm not, but I keep thinking that those kids who've been pawned off to caregivers could at least have a summer of fun." He chewed his lips and stared straight ahead as he brought together his thoughts. "What if we had a summer camp on Cass's property that she left to me? We could use the big house as the center and build bunkhouses for the kids." He turned to Speaker. "What do you think?"

"I like it! You could take them on the Wawanesa to swimming classes at the pier."

"Hawker could teach them canoeing and maybe you and he could take the older ones on a three or four-day canoe trip."

"We could set up targets for bow and arrows. I'm pretty good at that."

"Joe Big Canoe and his wife could come over from the reservation on the next island and teach crafts."

"I'm sure I could get Doc. Andrew to come and teach first aid and water safety."

"Elsa is really good at reading stories aloud."

"Clara could help with government paperwork."

The excitement of throwing one idea after another found they had arrived home unaware of the time that had flown by.

They pulled into the harbour and parked the truck but didn't get out immediately because George was saying, "We'll have to work all year to get it ready for next summer but there's one thing we have to do this summer."

"What's that?"

"Have a wedding for Bear and Elsa! I suspect they won't want anything to do with any of our churches after the fight over Frenchie."

"Who will marry them then?"

"We'll look into it."

Chapter 35

With elbows on the window sill of Elsa's apartment, Bear stared at the town hall across the street, where his office was waiting. Deep in thought, he wiped his fingers back and forth over his lips.

Can one be sure and unsure at the same time? When he came out of the anesthetic after being shot he realized how much he wanted and needed Elsa beside him. Now, every time she smiled he felt a burst in his chest, and when he woke with her comfortably spooned into his body, he knew that it was as it should be. It just was.

His leg still hurt—from time to time an electric pain shot through his groin, forcing him to collapse in a chair in agony. He knew the worst would pass, but it would leave him a lame small town cop. Is that what he wanted?

He thought of Jumper's telling photos which he hadn't yet destroyed. Already he was the keeper of secrets, and they would mount if he stayed in the job. And each tidbit of criminality that he held to his chest and didn't act on would weigh heavily. Even the knowing would make his approach to others more stilted. And what would he do if Speaker exercised his short temper and harmed someone, or if George stepped over the line? Were he to ignore it, he shouldn't be a cop. But then, perhaps being a small-town cop was different and could provide leeway for forgiveness.

To hell with it! He pushed himself from the chair and went down the stairs to join Elsa at the restaurant.

Bear hoisted himself on to his stool with care and pulled his leg in after him.

The restaurant was comfortably quiet. Elsa was behind the counter chopping vegetables; George had the Toronto Star spread out in front of him and Speaker was wiping off the coffee he had spilled on the front of the Cedartown express and trying to read between the stains. An elderly farm couple were digging into hamburgers, which, from the size of the pair was a modest part of their caloric intake. A teenaged boy and girl were tucked into a booth sipping coca colas and flirting quietly.

"Says here we're going to be able to pay all our bills with a piece of plastic!" George held his finger on the article.

"How?" Bear asked.

"Seems the plan is that you pay with the Diners Club Card, that's what it's called, and they pay you and get the money from a bank."

"You mean these Diners Club people will collect millions of bills we send them –figure it all out—send the money to everyone and then get it back from the bank?"

"Sounds impossible." Elsa stopped what she was doing, and came over to the counter. "Even if it did work, which I'm sure it won't, seems to me it would take a long time to get my money, and that could cause problems.

"I'll stick with the green stuff," Speaker added. He put his hand on the Express.

George shut and folded the newspaper. "Bear and Elsa, Speaker and I have something we want to suggest."

Elsa put down the cutlery she was drying and came from behind the counter to stand beside Bear who put his arm around her waist.

"We'd like to have your wedding party on Cass's property. We have the house, where food could be made and drinks could be served either inside or out. The Wawanesa could bring the guests over and the two of you could have the house for as many nights as you want." He smiled a tentative smile. 'What do you think?"

Bear turned to Elsa, lifted his eyebrows in a positive question and shrugged his shoulders, the gesture suggesting that it was up to Elsa.

"It sounds wonderful, boys, but what if there is bad weather?" Elsa asked.

"We thought of that," Speaker said sounding proud of their acumen. "We'll reserve the Legion Hall just in case!"

"But that would be too expensive," she insisted.

Speaker put his arm around George's shoulder. "Can't talk about money to my cousin. For him money is like shit stuck to the sole of his shoe."

"Thank you, then," she embraced each one, "It sounds wonderful!" She made her way back behind the counter, her eyes darting back and forth with questions. "What about the church ceremony? Were you thinking we would do that first and then get on the Wawanesa?"

"As you like, it's your wedding," George said. "What church? I didn't know you ever went."

"Not often, but I was christened in the Presbyterian Church, so I guess we'd have to ask Reverend Cameron to marry us."

"You'd let that holier-than-thou hypocrite marry you after what he did to Frenchie?" Speaker almost yelped.

"I can't see that we have a choice, they were all horrible to her".

A group of preteens piled into a booth and after flipping the pages of the juke box attached to the wall beside their table, chose The Andrews Sisters bellowing out "Don't Fence Me In," with them all singing along, creating an off-key cacophony.

"Hey, kids, switch to Nat King Cole or Bing Crosby so we can hear each other speak!" Bear called over his shoulder. "I'll pay for it."

Soon Nat King Cole came on.

"You made an impression," Elsa smiled.

"It was my offer to pay that did it." He took Elsa's hand. "Whatever you want to do is fine with me."

"Have you heard the man preach?" Speaker was upset. "He shouts and yells and pounds the pulpit. I went after I got out of prison thinking I'd become a better man if I paid more attention to the commandments, and he screamed directly at me and said my spirit and those of men like me, will be a burning carcass of sin forever in a torment of flames! I'm sorry Elsa but I can't go into that church ever again."

Elsa shrugged her shoulders and fought tears, "I hadn't thought it would be so difficult. Even though I respect the church and believe in

God, I never did have much use for God's messengers, but if we want to make it official we don't have any choice in the matter."

Speaker tore open his newspaper and pretended to read, while George and Bear sat quietly, each searching for options.

"There is another possibility." Bear sipped his coffee and put it down. "Judges can perform the marriage ceremony."

"Better than a Servant of God, I suppose but not a whole lot." Speaker grumbled.

"I don't know any judge, do any of you?" Elsa asked.

"I don't, but the Chief does and I'm sure he'd set it up for us." Bear said.

"Then you could have the whole ceremony on the island which would be wonderful!" George hurt his throat in announcing his pleasure.

"It would, wouldn't it?" Elsa agreed

Chapter 36

Wind smoothed the lake to a silver sheen and retreated, leaving Sun to hostess the event.

The Wawanesa was too large to dock at Cass's Place (forever to be known as such). So, the boats of various friends collected the guests at George's harbour and transferred them to the dock from where a path led through the woods to Cass's house.

George and Bear stood with their backs to the judge and waited as they all gathered on the open meadow, where some sat on boulders and others on benches Hawker had made from split logs.

"Nervous?" George asked.

"I am," Bear confessed.

"Not surprising," George answered. As well as marrying Beautiful Elsa he was marrying the town, and stepping into a new life with all the commitments that attended it. Change frightens.

"Is that really wedding music?" Bear gestured at Joe McPhee circumventing the crowd playing his pipes.

"Best we could get."

"A little wistful for a wedding, isn't it?"

"Just background. He'll come through with the wedding march in grand form, trust me."

"Who's the fat lady with two crutches?"

"That's Mira."

"THE MIRA? I'm finally going to meet THE MIRA?" Bear continued to smile and nod to everyone. Out of the side of his mouth he asked George, "How long is this going to take? What are we waiting for?"

"Speaker's bringing a special guest. Should be here any minute. There they are!"

"Frenchie!" Bear went to greet her with a hug. "You came all the way for this. I'm flattered, and very pleased to see you." He led her to a space on the log in the front of the gathering.

"When Speaker, he phoned me to tell me you and Elsa were marrying, I knew I must come to wish my friends well."

"Speaker has stayed in touch?" Bear was surprised.

"Oui! He's a good man, your friend. He phones a lot, like he is my protector."

"I didn't know, did you, George?"

George shook his head, equally surprised. He felt a honeyed pleasure at the thought of Speaker's quiet attention to Frenchie. He remembered how angry Speaker was when she was treated so badly, and this was his response. "He kept you entirely to himself," George smiled at Frenchie, "Nobody knew."

"Mira, she knew."

"Of course," he answered. Joe started playing the wedding march and George steered Bear back to the front where the two of them stood with their backs to the judge and watched Elsa appear on Speaker's arm. Carrying a simple bouquet of wildflowers, she was wearing a long straight white dress. Its simplicity permitting all the attention to rest on the beauty of her high-cheekbones and smiling full lips. Her dark-lashed eyes saw only Bear.

Achieving his responsibility with frowning seriousness, Speaker took her hand and placed it in Bear's. There were tears in his eyes as he stepped back.

"I was so nervous, I can't remember the ceremony," Elsa confessed happily.

"I don't remember a lot of it either, but I did hear you say 'I do'" Bear lifted her and swung her around in a circle. "The only words I needed to hear." He plunked her down and put his arm around her waist.

"Ladies and gentlemen." George croaked. May I present Mrs. Walter McKinley soon to be known as Mrs. Bear!"

Beaming with pleasure and not letting go of each other for a minute they moved among their friends accepting their good wishes.

Little Essie Fraser looked up and Elsa and said, "You are the most Gretel person in the whole world!"

Elsa bent down and gave her a kiss on the cheek. "Gretel?"

"Yes, you know, Handsome and Gretel!"

Affectionate smiles lit up all who overheard.

"Why thank you Essie, what a nice thing to say."

After the niceties of two hours of food and drink, people began to say their farewells, relying on Jack Winston to escort them to the mainland. Mrs. Fraser, who had her own boat took Essie by the hand and called to Tess. "It's time to go, Tess, we must leave these special friends who will find it easier to treasure the final drink without me."

"You're welcome to stay as long as you like, Mrs. Fraser, "Elsa insisted.

"Can we stay, Mother, please, please, can we stay?" Essie begged.

"No, it's time for us to go." She signaled to Tess who was no happier than her little sister, as Clara's son Michael was still there.

Bear went with her down the path to the dock.

She smiled her vague smile. "I imagine you are ours forever, now."

"What do you mean?"

"As the local law you'll be strapped with all the secrets of a small town."

"Are there a lot of secrets in Cedartown, Mrs. Fraser?"

"Oh my dear, yes. And it will often be difficult to know how to deal with them." Tess lifted Essie into the boat then helped her mother in, and went to sit in the front."

"You're not going to drive, Tess?" Bear asked.

"When mother's in the boat, mother drives," she announced with a touch of sarcasm.

Bear, pondering, returned to his friends. He arrived to hear Clara asking Frenchie, "How is it back in your town? Have you been accepted?"

"It is fine. I see my friends and family who treat me like gauze-covered wound that they can see through and feel sorry about."

"They're mistake." Speaker's voice rose.

Frenchie took his hand and patted it. "Per'aps you are right but it is o.k. I don't drink anymore and I don't stink of shit."

Speaker shook his head refusing to accept her explanation.

George leaned against the kitchen counter and absorbed the various conversations.

"Mira," Bear sat down beside her. "I should have made an effort to go and meet you in person. I feel as though I know you. You are a recurring thought for me, not only when you saved my life by calling the ambulance for me, but in all the other instance you've helped." He touched her hand. "Your words have saved hundreds, and never once hurt. I bet you hold back as often as you give, and for that, you really do deserve an award!"

"To Mira," Speaker said, and raised his glass.

"To Mira!!" They all stood and repeated in unison.

Her large body was ensconced in the depths of the easy chair. She fiddled with her crutches. "It's the same for me. I know you all but have only imagined your faces,"

"Have they matched our voices?" Elsa asked.

"Of course not!" Mira laughed at herself. I knew you women of course, you, Elsa, and Clara and Alice have all visited but not the men. How was I to know that Bear was huge with such a gentle voice or that George was so handsome when he sounds like a bullfrog?

"I visited you more than any of them," Speaker insisted.

"Of course you did," she smiled affectionately, "Without me you would have no idea which of your lady friends lived where, or even their last names."

Speaker wiped back the hair that had fallen over his forehead and smiled an embarrassed smile.

The teasing continued. "You can't even remember their names, Speaker?" "Which one was it that had the angry father go after you with a gun?" "You'd better have Mira tell you the name of whoever you were seeing that night!'

When he saw his cousin's smile wavering Gorge leaped in to change the conversation. "I've been thinking about what to do with this property and Speaker and I have played around with the idea of creating a summer camp for foster kids. What do you think?"

The response elicited a noisy excitement They were so full of ideas his friends couldn't sit still, and one jumped up to talk over another, each volunteering to participate. George sat back enjoying the excited suggestions of these good human beings. With an absent smile. he looked out over the miles of gentle ripples that mothered his island, his home. Memories, my Cass, need to be tucked away. I need to get on with the future. With a silent nod, he bid farewell to the only woman he ever loved.

Mira brought her bulk forward and leaned her chin on a crutch. "There's something else going on around here I think you should know." Her tone did not promise good news.

They all waited.

"A developer is negotiating to purchase Prevost Point with the intention of building a hotel and a harbour."

"But that's Hawker's land," Speaker insisted.

"I think my father, he didn't buy it, we just lived there." Hawker said from the kitchen where he was helping Alice clean up so as to leave the house in good shape for the newlyweds.

"You sure?" George asked.

"Maybe sure, don't know," Hawker looked off in the air seeming to search for an answer.

"We can certainly find out by going through the town records," Clara said. "But the big question is, "George and Speaker, what do you think about having a hotel on the island? It would change your life the most."

"It's uncomfortable, but we're dreaming if we think we can keep things as they are forever." George's rough voice had a soulful ring to it. "We can't harness change. The best we can do is let go of what is, and try to control what's to come."

"How do we do that?" Speaker asked.

"Join the dance. Make sure it is done legally and well."

"And if it isn't?" Speaker asked.

"Then we'll raise Holy Hell!" George laughed.

After two wonderful nights at Cass's Place, Elsa rolled over in bed, kissed Bear's back and whispered, "I could stay here for weeks, but poor

Alice has been left with the restaurant so, much as I hate it, I'll have to go back."

Bear turned over and enveloped her in a hug. "It's best to leave when everything is perfect." He kissed her forehead. "I have things to do as well."

"There's something on your mind, I can tell."

"An unanswered question I have to chase."

Elsa rolled over on top of him. "Then let's have a finale to our perfect memory."

Back in Cedartown, Bear found a lot of work awaiting him, but he couldn't hold back his visit for another day.

At Mrs. Fraser's house, Tess was sitting in a deck chair with a book lying open on her lap. At the sound of Bear's approach, she opened one eye. "Oh, hi Bear," she greeted him without enthusiasm.

Bear looked down at seductive girl/child. He could have destroyed his relationship with Malcolm and the respect of George, to say nothing of his opinion of himself had George not saved him. A knock on his door was all that saved him. He would be forever grateful to George. "Where's your Mom, Tess?"

"With eyes closed, she waved her hand towards the house. "Inside somewhere."

Bear smiled as he turned towards the house, damned sure that the girl/child's reaction screamed pride in lost virginity. Suggesting to Michael, Clara's son, that he look into assisting at the swimming classes, was an obvious success.

Bear found Mrs. Fraser sitting in the living room flipping through a photo album. She didn't get up and looked at him with a vague smile.

"Mrs. Fraser." Bear sat in the chair opposite her without asking.

She leaned into the page of the album to see a photo more closely. Without looking up she replied, "What can I do for you Bear?"

"Something you said to me at my wedding: that I would have to live with the secrets of Cedartown."

"I did say that, didn't I?"

"What did you mean?"

She put her hands together, placed them on the album and looked him squarely in the face. "I meant, the responsibilities of a small-town policeman often necessitate ignoring the law."

"I'm not sure I understand."

"Friendship and secrets come first in a place like this,"

Bear leaned his elbow on the arm of his chair, rested his chin on his fist, and after a lengthy silence said, "You killed Jumper, didn't you?"

"I did." There was no guilt in the affirmation. "He killed my husband."

"How did you do it?"

"I'd been keeping an eye on the despicable creature, ever since the funeral, waiting for the appropriate moment. When he set up his camera in the overgrowth on the tip of the opposing wall of the pier I simply walked along the path with my hammer and hit him on the head while he was concentrating on taking a photo of some nefarious happening on the other side." She smiled and looked away. "It wasn't difficult."

"How did you get him into the lake?"

"Oh, I pulled him through the tall weeds and left him there until I fetched my boat. Then, with a rope tied under his arms I towed him well out into the lake." She put her album aside and pushed herself up from the chair. After smoothing her skirt, she said, "I think I got as much pleasure dumping his dreaded camera as I did ridding the world of him."

Bear stood when she did.

She took his arm, "I'll see you out."

Bear didn't move. "And the soldier who accosted Essie?"

"I found him on the railway bridge. He was drunk. All I had to do was push." She urged him towards the door. "Of course, there is nothing you can or will do about any of it."

In a daze, Bear let her urge him towards the door.

In the car, he let his head fall against the steering wheel. "Now what do I do?"

Printed in the United States
by Baker & Taylor Publisher Services